Avarice

Pyrrh Considerable Crimes Division: Book One

ANNIE BELLET

Cover designed by Greg Jensen with art by Nathie
Copyright 2012

Formatting by Polgarus Studio

ISBN-13: 978-1482325027
ISBN-10: 1482325020

CHAPTER ONE

Akil reached the square just as the second bell rang in Kassim's Tower and a light rain started falling. His heart beat fiercely in his chest. Above him a street lamp flickered, its chemicals fading. He slipped a gold coin, one of the heavy suns, from his pouch and forced himself to breathe evenly. One more payment. After tonight, it would be over. His lover, Jala, would be happy and they'd be free to start over.

He looked up at the guttering lamp. It was one of the globes that all alchemical apprentices made far too many of in their first years. The thick glass ball was nearly empty of glowing liquid, only residue staining its sides. He knew the formula by heart. Akil whispered the words to himself, closing his eyes for a moment as he rubbed chilled fingers over the coin in his hand. *Phosphor, Moon's Bane, Ember-tail Ant Venom.*

The sound of horses' hooves on the stones drew Akil from his nervous reverie. A hackney carriage passed by, the hooded driver hunched in the rain, carrying with him a pool of light from the swinging lanterns. The hack went through the square and turned the corner, heading out of Old Town and toward the University of Science and Alchemy.

Akil's breath misted in the chilly spring air and he pulled the collar of his wool coat up and hunched his shoulders. While he understood the need for a quiet, out-of-the-way meeting for such unsavory business, the middle of the night cloak-and-dagger feel of this particular location and time felt overly dramatic.

The man he was meeting did not have a dramatic flair. Something was off. It couldn't be good. He shifted from one foot to the other and touched his breast pocket. The papers were still there, his ticket to a new life reassuring him.

Footsteps and then movement in the shadows cast by the flickering light as someone walked along the edge of the square, moving past a closed shop front.

"Zer?" Akil called out. *Let's get this done, no more games.*

Footsteps closer, running, then right behind him.

Something sharp dug into his back and pain exploded in little red dots across his vision. The figure ahead of him stepped into the light.

"But I..." Akil started to say but his mouth wouldn't work. Another sharp pain, then another, and Akil felt someone behind him stepping aside even as he collapsed to the ground. Sickening waves washed over him and his body started to shake. A shadow loomed above and he saw a dagger descending toward his chest.

Akil put his arms up but they moved as though the air had become syrup. Fire lanced through his forearms as the dagger slashed his sleeves. The blade bit into his chest and his heart stopped pounding so loudly in his ears.

Still clutched in his fingers, the coin dug into his palm. He had his purpose here. Akil fought to think through the pain as the dagger thrust into his chest again. He felt the warm breath of the man above him but couldn't focus his eyes to see his killer's face. It didn't matter. He knew why he was dying.

Akil shoved his fist into his mouth, his bloody lips closing over the coin. *Damn you all to Anunnaki*, he thought as the hard metal lodged in the back of his throat. Darkness closed in over him, pain turning to cold, and then the cold turned to nothingness.

CHAPTER TWO

Zhivana muttered a curse as ink splashed across the bottom of the final form. She dumped sand over the mess and impatiently poured it off into a tray before gathering up the papers and shoving them onto the clerk's desk.

"Done," she said, forcing herself not to bare her teeth at the little human bureaucrat. It wasn't his fault that her transfer papers hadn't made it over to the Pyrrh Considerable Crimes Division yet. Thanks to paperwork, she was late for work on her first day.

"Third floor," the clerk said and motioned to the stairs. "You need a temporary badge?"

She jerked her badge out of her shirt and showed the heavy medallion to him, the red-gold sheen painfully bright and new. "I'm good, thanks," she growled.

She took the stairs two at a time, one hand steadying her short sword so it didn't bang her leg.

The sun was coming up and morning light streamed in through the tall, narrow windows. The stairs ended in a hallway that branched off to three doors. She'd been assigned to the Grave Squad, the Cordonates who investigated serious crimes reported during the late night and early morning hours.

There was no door, just a brass plaque on the right, next to the opening, that read "Grave". Some wise-ass had scratched "peril" in rough, blocky letters beneath.

Zhivana started toward that opening but stopped as her keen hearing picked up voices.

"They're assigning her to Par?" A male voice, probably human, said.

"Guess so. Word is she's as crazy as he is." Another, younger-sounding, male voice.

"Eridu help her, she's got to be. Turning down a Captaincy and the fat pension she'd get in few years for *this* gig? She's almost thirty. That gives her what, another five years before retirement?"

Zhivana flattened her ears to her head and took a deep breath. Clearly she was going to have an interesting time with her new coworkers. But she'd expected it would be tough at first. Her starting days in the City Watch hadn't been all soft cheese and fluffy biscuits either.

"She's that kirgani who scaled the Sea Gate, I think."

Eavesdropping wasn't going to help and it certainly wasn't making her less late. She sighed and stepped into the doorway. The room was wide open with a half circle of desks in it. Hanging on the walls were slate and corkwood boards with various case details tacked up or scrawled on them. There were two scribe stations, unmanned. At the back was another door with a plaque on it. The room smelled of chalk and sweat and freshly steeped tea. Her stomach twisted and reminded her that she'd been too nervous to eat that morning.

"Yes," she said, smiling without baring her sharp teeth. "Scaled it and fell right into the drink."

The two men were both human and somewhere in their middle age, though one was going grey at the temples with what hair he had left. He wore a dark brown vest over a plain linen shirt. The other was dressed almost as a dandy, with a brocade coat unbuttoned over tailored trousers and a laced-front shirt in pale blue. Both had daggers at their waists but no swords or bows. Both had the same open-mouthed look.

She didn't recognize either of them. Zhivana walked forward, glad that at least she'd dressed appropriately. She'd been told that Cordonates wore whatever they liked while on the job, but it felt strange to be out of her russet and green uniform after all these years. She had brought her sword, though, since the Cordonates she'd worked with had all carried weapons. It was a comfortable, familiar weight at her hip.

"Zhivana Nedrogovna," she said, extending one six-fingered hand, careful to keep her claws sheathed. "I'm looking for the Lieutenant."

"Mikal Antar," said the older man, recovering faster than his younger partner. He took her offered arm, clasping forearms with her. His brown skin was smooth and warm beneath her palm, his grip strong but not overpowering. He looked her right in the eye and gave a little nod.

"I'm Qays Narzari," the other one said, slipping off the desk he'd been perched on and extending his own hand. His fingers brushed her fur and his hazel eyes widened a little. Zhivana guessed he hadn't touched many Kirgani before. "Everyone, eh, calls me Keen." His voice carried a slight lilt to it, as though he'd trained himself out of the sing-song of the streets.

The door at the back of the room opened and the tallest human Zhivana had ever seen stepped out, ducking to avoid the lintel. He had skin that was so dark it blended with the collar of his black vest, and tiny braids along his skull that ended in bright yellow threads. Apparently the Lieutenant was a devotee of the god Enlil, Protector of the Helpless and Lord of Storms. She automatically filed that information away in her mind.

"Sorry I'm late, zer Hajjar," she said, stepping away from the others. She had never met him either, but she had asked around and gotten a description of her new superior.

"No excuse?" He raised an eyebrow.

Zhivana shook her head. What was the point of excuses? Words wouldn't change facts.

"Good." He smiled and his teeth were almost translucent. "Your partner is not here. You've caught a case, but Par didn't feel like waiting around when we weren't sure how long the clerks would keep you."

Wormshit. First day and already she was way behind. She opened her mouth but the Lieutenant held up his hand.

"The body is just on the other side of the Sciences district. The corpse cart is heading out any moment. You can catch a ride with the medical examiner's assistants." Hajjar jerked his head toward the door. "If you hurry."

Their throaty chuckles followed her out of the room and down the stairs.

Angry voices pierced the chill morning as they approached the crime scene. A small crowd of onlookers blocked the old stone street as the wagon turned into a market square just under the shadow of Kassim's belltower. The sixth bell finished ringing as Zhivana jumped free of the cart and sprinted down the road. She had her hand crossbow out of its sheath and loaded with a sleep dart on reflex.

She passed two uniformed Watch officers who should have been helping secure the scene but instead stood gaping along with the little crowd of early morning shopkeepers and craftsmen. Next to a lamppost lay what she assumed was the body, though it was covered by a cloth, forming a tragic lump in the road.

The yelling came from a young human male in a loose shirt and black leather breeches. He had shoved a portly, older human male – who from his worn leather apron she guessed was a shop keeper,– up against a shuttered shop, and was punctuating his angry questions with fists to the belly.

"Tell me what you took, you gormless bastard," the assaulting male said.

Zhivana stopped a few yards off and raised her bow. The angry idiot could sleep off the drugs and then answer some questions at the division house. She wondered where in the nineteen hells her new partner was.

Then the younger man shifted and she saw his CCD medallion swinging on its chain. Parshan Kouri. She froze for a moment, and then jammed her bow back into its holder. A few quick steps took her to him just as he raised his fist for another blow to the beleaguered shopkeeper's sternum. She grabbed his arm and wrenched him away, using her shorter but more muscular bulk to press him backward.

Moss-green eyes glared at her and his other hand went for his sword. Zhivana shoved him hard and he slammed backward into the building.

"You're under arrest, ratling," he growled.

"I'm not under arrest," she said. Her hackles rose but she forced her tone to stay mild. "Nor am I a ratling. I'm your new partner, *partner*."

The anger died in his eyes and she felt the tension go out of him as his hand dropped from his sword hilt, letting the blade slide back into the sheath. He reached up with one hand and tugged on his ponytail. He had a broad face with about a day's worth of dark beard growing in and he carried a shadow in his expression as though he'd woken to some private grief.

In the corner of her vision, Zhivana saw the shopkeeper sliding along the wall, clearly thinking about leaving.

"Stick around," she said, turning toward him. And then to her partner, "What's the story here?"

He recovered his composure quickly, she'd give him that. One glance at the CCD badge hanging from her own neck and he stood up straighter, taking a deep breath.

"Body's picked clean. This guy found him, says he found it that way. But I don't like his answers." Parshan motioned at the shopkeeper and stepped forward again.

The corpse wagon had pulled up and the medical examiner's assistant stood by. Though she didn't recognize her, Zhivana smiled approval at the Watch officer who took the initiative and started waving people back.

"All right," she said and stepped forward to the shopkeeper, pulling a slim pad of paper and an inkstone nub from her vest. "Name?"

"Dhul... , uh... , Dhul Fiqar. That's my shop there." He pointed at the door of a butcher's shop kitty-corner from where they stood. "I swear he was like that when I found him. I'm the one that called the gree-, er, the Watch." He caught himself with an embarrassed, nervous laugh before using the slang term "greenie".

"I warn you, zer Fiqar," Zhivana said, "we Kirgani can smell lies." She twitched her whiskers for emphasis and he flinched.

"He was dead," Fiqar said, spreading his hands out.

Zhivana put her arm out and caught Parshan across the chest, stopping him from grabbing the shopkeeper again.

"Hand over whatever you took." She let the mildness drain out of her voice.

Defeated, Fiqar reached into one of the deep pockets in his apron and pulled out a bracelet and a chain with a Guild apprentice's silver medallion hanging from it. "That's all he had. No purse or anything, I swear. Can I go to my shop now? I need to open."

It would be a pain in the arse to pull him in on theft charges, and she didn't relish the thought of doing more paperwork so soon. Zhivana shrugged. Parshan reached past her and took the pieces. "Don't go far."

Zhivana turned and they peered at the apprentice's medallion. It bore the etching of a set of scales and a beaker on one side with the High Lord's profile and a stylized "T" on the other. Carefully-stamped lettering read "Gerges". The bracelet was city issue, a citizen tag that had the same name, adding "Akil" and with a number that should, if they were lucky, correspond to paperwork listing kin and address in the Hall of Records.

"Alchemist's Guild, office of the treasury. Interesting." Zhivana looked at her partner. "I'm Zhivana, by the way."

"Parshan. Par," he said with a slight grimace that she guessed would be all the apology she'd get for his earlier words. He didn't offer to clasp arms, but his hands were full as he fished a small pouch out of his belt and shoved the bracelet and identification into it.

"You two wanna look at this guy before I move him?" The ME's assistants stood by with a stretcher; one, who'd introduced herself to Zhivana as Almas, tapping her foot on the corner of the canvas covering the victim.

"Sure," Par said.

Zhivana pulled on her thin leather gloves and rolled her shoulders. No matter how many dead bodies she'd seen, it never seemed to get easier. But getting down to her job calmed her nerves. This is what she'd wanted. For too many years she'd been the uniformed bystander charged with crowd control and reporting. She'd wanted to catch the worst criminals, not just drag tax dodgers in on fines or collar the occasional petty thief. She wanted the murderers, the rapists, the worst of the scum. Corpses were just part of the job.

This one, the unfortunate zer Gerges, wasn't pretty. The rain the night before had washed off a lot of the blood and kept the smell down, but he looked damn dead. He was a young, human male. Zhivana wasn't good at estimating human ages, but she doubted the man was much older than she. He wore a waistcoat heavily torn and stained with blood over shabby trousers that were missing a belt. His eyes were bugged out and clouded over and his jaw clenched shut, giving him an angry expression.

"Defensive wounds. Robbery, probably." Par snorted. "Maybe he was drunk. Stupid to be wandering around Old Town unarmed in the middle of the night."

Zhivana crouched next to the body and gently shifted him. There were a lot of stab wounds. "Dagger or a big knife. ME will be able to tell us more. I don't know if this was a mugging."

Par folded his arms across his chest and looked for a moment as though he'd argue with her. Zhivana wondered if his first reaction to anything was to pick a fight. This was going to be one interesting partnership if that was the case. But he bent over and looked at the body more closely, sucking air in and out between his teeth in an annoying whistle that would have been inaudible to a human.

She was willing to put coin on him knowing the sound would bug her.

"You're right," he said, his eyes flicking to her. "Too many wounds. No need to stab so many times just to get a purse. And why not take his bracelet and the apprentice silver?"

She tucked her fingers under the body and rolled the corpse gently. "Stabbed in the back, probably first judging from how he fell, though the killer could have rolled him." She straightened up and looked at how the body was positioned. If he'd fallen backward, as it appeared he had, he'd been facing down the street, standing beneath the lamp.

"He was waiting for someone," Zhivana said, pointing at the lamp. "He stood here so he could be seen. This had to be personal."

"Clothes are wet. He died either before or during last night's rainfall."

Zhivana sniffed around the body. "No point calling in trackers. Rain took care of any scent trail. Not sure what else we can do here. Did the Watch question bystanders? No witnesses?"

"Just the shopkeeper. No one was around when this guy went down. No one who'll come forward, anyway. No residences on this street." Par straightened up and called out to a driver perched on a CCD cart in the square. "Faris, let's go." He jingled the pouch with the victim's remaining valuables. "Shall we head over to the treasury office and see what we can learn about this unfortunate sot?"

"You can take him," Zhivana said to Almas. She smiled with lots of teeth at her partner and climbed up into the hack as Faris pulled it around. "I'm in the mood to make a bureaucrat's day a little more interesting."

CHAPTER THREE

Par sat on the wooden seat of the hack and tried not to stare too overtly at his new partner. He'd been annoyed when Lt. Hajjar had summarily informed him he was getting someone new. It felt too damn soon to be replacing Kalja. It would always feel too soon.

And replacing her with a kirgani no less. Zhivana was a strange one. Some kirgani served in the City Watch, but none had ever applied to be in the CCD before, least not as a Cordonate. It took a lot of years of beat patrol to even earn the right to apply, and the short-lived kirgani didn't generally put in the time or show any inclination to do more than serve and pension out for the last decade or so of their lives. Zhivana had almost made Watch Captain, if the rumors were true. She had ambition, drive.

And she was funny-looking. Calico – all orange and black and cream like a house cat – instead of the more common black-and-silver or varied brown fur pattern. Her eyes were unnerving as well, a depthless blue that shifted with the light like open water. She was compact and plain otherwise, eschewing the jewelry and piercings her kind often wore.

Par sucked in his breath and looked away as she flicked her odd eyes to him and her whiskers twitched. She was no damn Kalja, but he didn't have a choice. At least she seemed solid enough and hadn't lost her breakfast over the corpse or done anything stupid.

Unlike him. His fists clenched on his thighs. So stupidly difficult to get a hold of the rage inside lately. It washed through his blood at the slightest provocation, begging for an outlet, preferably a violent one. He shouldn't have slammed that shopkeeper against the wall, but the moment the man started obviously lying, Par's good sense had burned right out of his mind. No way in the seventeen hells of Apirictim was he going to apologize though. Screw first impressions.

He just needed to focus, to solve this case. It would be good to get a solve on a case involving someone from the Treasury. This was the sort of thing that would help Hajjar see that Par was fine. If only he could convince himself so easily.

His eyes shifted back to Zhivana. She'd either help or not. He didn't need a partner, but if she wanted to be useful, he wouldn't stop her. If she expected him to be friendly she was in for a nasty shock. Par would do his damn job. No more chatter, no more caring, no more getting attached to anything.

His bitter thoughts rode with them up to the steps of the High Lord's Administrative Works building. The white marble façade and ribbed columns gleamed in the weak morning sun. Other carriages were coming and going in the loop of road out front, bureaucrats in jackets and gowns and apprentice robes climbing out and ascending the steps to begin the work day. Behind the building loomed the hill of the Noble District and the towers of the High Lord's Palace, still swathed in the morning mists coming off the sea.

The Office of the Treasury took up about a quarter of the second floor. A hassled-looking, middle-aged woman in a dark grey dress with a very unfashionable high-necked bodice looked up from a pile of papers she was sorting as Par and Zhivana pushed through the large double doors.

"If you have an appointment," she said, staring at them with skepticism, "no one else is likely to be in for another bell at least."

Zhivana reached into her shirt to get her badge but Par stepped forward and held up his own.

"Do you know someone named Akil Gerges?" he asked as the woman's eyes widened.

"Yes? Apprentice, err, I mean Journeyman Akil Gerges. He works for Fawzi Batros, in the alchemy office, lower level. Is there a problem?"

"When was he promoted?" Zhivana asked as Par opened the pouch holding Gerges's medallion and tags.

"Last week." The woman ran a shaky hand through her iron grey hair, mussing her bun. "Is there a problem?" she repeated. "Gerges and Batros won't be in for a while."

"Gerges won't be in ever again," Par said. He held out the medallion and watched her flinch in recognition. "He's dead."

The secretary sat down into her carved wood chair with a heavy thunk. "Oh dear. How? Nevermind. I don't... Has his family been, I mean, do they know?"

"That's why we're here. Do you have an address for him? Or for any kin?" Par said. Zhivana had her little paper pad and inkstone out, annoyingly efficient. He didn't bother to get out his own. If his new partner wanted to play scribe, she could knock herself out.

"His mother lives somewhere in Old Town, I think. But he has a lover, who is... , one second," she said, pulling open a drawer on the wall of dark wood cabinets behind her. She flipped through sheets of fine, creamy paper and pulled one out. "Jala Kawthar. She is Akil's emergency contact. Murksor Square, building seven-two-eight, Sciences district."

Par bit his tongue and resisted, barely, snidely asking Zhivana if she'd got all that. "Thank you," he muttered instead to the secretary. "When will zi Batros be in? We might need to come back and talk to him."

"Between half-seven and eight, usually."

Zhivana followed him out of the offices after thanking the secretary again. They climbed back up into the hack and Par gave Faris the address. So much of this job was just riding around in carts. He wished the CCD would at least shell out the coin for a better sprung rig, but wishes were about as useful as dust when it came to budgets.

"You could work on your manner," Zhivana said to him. "I've no fondness for clerks either, but you broke the news like smashing a brick through a window."

Par lifted his head and felt his fists clench again as rage tickled his veins and turned his belly sour. Two deep breathes brought the killing impulse under control enough to respond.

"You want me to offer her a cup of tea? Or a hug? This is the job, puppy. We don't solve murders by holding hands."

"My name is Zhivana. Not 'puppy.' Not 'kitten.' Not 'ratling.' Do I need to kick your ass to make this clear?" All her teeth gleamed at him as she drew back her lips. She had very nice, white, sharp teeth.

"Try it." The tingling started in his hands and his heart calmed as the rage shivered over him.

"Hey! Both of you, for bloody Ningal's sake, cut it out." Faris pulled up on the reins, causing a cabbage carter behind them to yell out some choice obscenities as she was forced to pull up short behind the hack.

"To be continued," Zhivana muttered. "We'll behave. Drive on."

Par snorted and slowly forced his palms open, rubbing them on his pants. Damn Hajjar for pairing him up so soon. And damn Kalja for dying.

And damn him, damn himself most of all, for being too much of a coward to save her.

Zhivana grabbed Par's arm as they reached the door for seven-two-eight. He spun and glared at her, shaking off her hand. Rage burned inside his moss-green eyes, bright and clear. She backed off a step, wondering why he wanted to kill somebody so badly.

"Heyla," she said, forcing her hackles down. This was not the time to dish out the much-needed ass-kicking. If he wanted to play angry male with her, she'd deal. He wasn't the first human to posture and spill hate all over her just for her being what she was. "This is Gerges's lover. We should probably be a little more tactful when we tell her. She'll have a hard enough time later when she comes to ident the body."

Muscles jumped in his jaw but he let out his breath and shrugged. "Sure. Unless she killed him, in which case we're playing fools."

"Innocent until we can find enough witnesses saying otherwise," she said, trying for a little Watch humor.

"I'll play nice." For a moment a tiny smile flickered at the corner of his mouth, but he pressed it out with a snort and turned away.

Par banged on the heavy door while Zhivana looked around. The building was typical of the Sciences district townhomes. Nice, clean neighborhood; double-story, brown brick houses buttressing a large, triangle-shaped central area that boasted a small fountain burbling in the background. Carriages rolled by and a few pedestrians stared at them curiously as they headed out of the surrounding homes.

A very pregnant human woman opened the door after the second bout of knocking. She was young for a human, in her twenties, with soft brown hair spilling over her robed shoulders. She clutched the night dress shut over her bulging belly and blinked at them.

"Jala Kawthar?" Par said, holding up his badge. She nodded. "We're with CCD and we need to talk to you about Akil Gerges. May we come in?" He added the last part with a glance back to Zhivana as if to say "see how good I'm being?"

"Akil's not here," she said, her voice rough but soft. "I think he left for work early."

"Please, zira. Let us in and we'll sort this out," Zhivana said. Par was already pushing his way past the confused woman and Zhivana sighed. Good manners only stuck so much, apparently.

They half followed, half led Jala into her own sitting parlor. The place looked like thieves had hit it and been less than particular in what they took. The only furniture was a large settee carved from walnut, upholstered in horsehide and old enough that the fur had rubbed off in parts. It was a masculine piece, the effect ruined by the two pillows resting on it, edged with lace and embroidered with pink and green flowers.

The room smelled heavily of tea roses and disturbed dust. Zhivana resisted the urge to cover her sensitive nose and looked for the dust's source. The shelves built into one wall were nearly empty of knickknacks and the surfaces had been wiped recently, though not thoroughly. The lone fireplace was clear of charcoal, even in the chill, spring morning. Two large trunks sat beside the doorway as though waiting for someone to pick them up and carry them away.

"Going somewhere?" Par asked.

"Yes. I mean, what's this about? Akil must be at work. Did someone commit a crime?" She twisted her hands and looked between them, not inviting either to sit.

"Why would you say that?" Zhivana said.

"Akil's mother," she answered quickly, her large brown eyes blinking. "She's a poppy addict. Is she in trouble?"

"Sit down, Jala," Par said.

Something in his voice got to her and she moved between them and sat heavily on the settee, clutching one of the pillows to her ample chest.

Zhivana looked at Par. She'd made a few notifications during her time in the Watch, but it wasn't something she'd ever gotten used to. While she was sure Jala was hiding something, she didn't figure the hugely pregnant woman would have been out in the middle of the night stabbing her lover on a rainy street. For one, it had only been a few bells since his death, and there was no way she'd done all the packing here just in the early morning.

"Akil is dead," Par said, spreading his hands almost in apology.

"What? Are you sure? I just saw him last night. We…" she trailed off, her shoulders shaking and eyes wide as Par pulled the apprentice medallion from his pouch again.

"We'll need you to come down to the CCD building and identify the body to be sure." Par took the silver back from her shaking fingers as she stared mutely into space.

"Was he, I mean, how? How?" Jala's teeth made sharp dents in her lower lip as she wrapped her arms around her belly and started to rock back and forth.

Zhivana sighed. She'd see the body. No point sugaring this up anymore than was necessary. "He was murdered, stabbed. In Old Town. Did he go out last night?"

Jala shook her head, avoiding their eyes. "He went to bed with me. But he was gone when I got up. I assumed to work. Oh gods."

"You didn't notice him getting up in the night?" Par's tone was laced with skepticism and Zhivana contemplated hitting him. It would ruin the show of solidarity and professionalism, so she added this to her growing list of things to deck him for later.

"I take special teas for the baby. They make me sleep heavily. I don't usually see him in the mornings."

"Would anyone have wanted to hurt Akil? A dispute at work or among your friends?" Zhivana pulled out her notebook and forced her tone to stay even and calm.

"His mother was unhappy about us moving. I mean." Jala's eyes flicked up at them and she swallowed audibly. "Me moving in with him. She thinks the baby will be the end of him giving her money for... her habit."

"Work?"

Jala's face grew even paler and she hiccupped. Her eyes stared past Zhivana as though seeing something in the distance. Par cleared his throat as though he were going to speak but then the widow answered.

"No, work was going well. He just made Journeyman, before his thirtieth birthday. Akil is very good. Was. Oh." She started to sob again, big tears leaking from her eyes.

"You said you're moving in with him? So not here? Does he have another residence?" Par folded his arms and looked utterly uncomfortable. Zhivana guessed that he'd rather be out punching people than talking to sobbing widows. She hoped he was good at the punching, because so far he didn't seem overly competent at the other parts of this job.

Guiltily she admonished herself to give him more of a chance than just the space of a bell.

"Yes, he has a place over on Scill Crossing, on the other side of the University. Nine-five-zero-zero, upper floor." The words tumbled out as though they'd been rehearsed. Jala stared down at her hands, at the pillow, at the pale blue gown stretched over her belly, carefully looking at everything but either of them.

"We might have more questions for you when you come down to the CCD building," Zhivana said, stalling Par with a shake of her head. More trauma wouldn't get them different answers. She judged it was better to let the woman calm down a little and absorb the truth of her situation before they pressed her further.

"Do I have to go now? Can I bring someone? I don't want to do this alone." Jala finally looked up, her brown eyes full of tears.

"A friend is a good idea," Zhivana said. The woman looked hardly able to breathe, much less stand on her own.

"Come by before thirteen bells," Par said at the same time.

"Yes, I will. I'll come." She didn't rise to see them out, but called after them as they turned away. "Old town? You said he was found in Old Town?"

"Yes?" Zhivana said, turning back, ears pricked.

"Off Overlook? His mother lives in that area, if you haven't located her yet. Nansilla Gerges. I don't know her exact address, she moves around."

"Thank you, Jala," Zhivana said, smiling without teeth. "If there's anything you need or remember, just tell the clerk at the main desk down at CCD that you need to talk to Cordonate Nedragovna. We'll see you later."

The moment the heavy wooden door had closed behind them, Par wheeled around and the glare was back.

"Swallow it," Zhivana said as she brought up her hands and unsheathed her claws. "I don't know what your problem is, whether you're a racist bastard or because you resent having your dead partner replaced, or what-have-you. I don't give three shits about it. I'm here to solve a murder so that people like that woman in there can have some closure in their lives and so justice, such as it bloody is, gets done."

His face went pale and he froze with his lips half open. Zhivana couldn't even hear him breathing over the sound of her own angry pulse.

"Fair enough," he said after a long moment. She could have sworn a glint of humor shone in his flat green eyes for a scant moment. "Widow's hiding things. Not sure how important, yet."

"Everyone is hiding something." Zhivana relaxed her tense shoulders and let her claws slip back into their sheaths.

She still wanted to scream and rip the hell out of this incomprehensible human, but she could be big enough to take the peace extended. The isolation of this new position hit her all at once and sucked the last fight from her body. Even though she'd been always aloof, a little separate from her cohorts, both by race and in rank, she'd had friends in the Watch. With the CCD, she was a baby again, starting over, and she felt the acute lack of anyone watching her back.

"Maybe there's something useful at the victim's place. Do we need an official writ to enter?" She turned and followed Par as he jumped up into the cart.

"Nah. Getting murdered pretty much gives us free rein on his place as long as we record anything we take as evidence." Par shrugged. "Faris, to Scill Crossing."

Scill Crossing turned out to be one of the winding back streets that crisscrossed the Sciences district as little more than a series of alleys, looping around the large stone buildings of the University of Science and Alchemy. The CCD cart turned off a main through-way and onto a narrow street shadowed by illegally built balconies hanging precariously from three and four story apartments. Refuse piles lined the uneven cobbles, missed by the morning street cleaners, and beggars lurked under the eaves, tying on their disguises for the day's work.

Somewhere beyond this dingy road, Zhivana heard a fiddler busquing, playing a sped-up version of "Nine Ladies in the Bower". It did little to cheer the area.

"Nice place," Par muttered, climbing down.

"Just the sort of spot I'd raise a child in." Zhivana did cover her nose this time. The air was helped by a cool sea wind curling in over the far cliffs, but the stench of human refuse permeated everything as they approached the rickety wooden steps leading to the second level of the building with nine-five-zero-zero carved into a wooden sign on its front.

"Fire trap." Par kicked at a loose board that was pretending to be a part of the narrow landing. "Jala's story's falling apart here."

He tried the door, pushing on the worn brass handle. It swung open. Zhivana had been looking out across the narrow alley into covered windows of the house across the way. The twang of a bowstring caught her ears and she jerked around. There was no time to think. She grabbed Par and shoved the big human through the door, knocking him to his knees.

The crossbow bolt missed him, slicing into her left arm near the shoulder before flying askew. She had her own handbow out as quick as breathing and leapt over her partner. Two men stood in the one-room apartment, both armed with knives that glinted in the dim light coming through the one grimy window.

She drew her sword and brought up the bow, aiming for the nearest man. Par stumbled to his feet behind her, bumping against the back of her calf. Her dart went wide.

The first man, a lanky human with a large nose that looked like a ship's hull smashed on rocks, charged at them, crouching low with his blade in a reverse grip. Zhivana ducked to the side before she realized that was what he'd intended. She twisted, bringing her sword up into guard but the man had already engaged with Par.

The second intruder, his face obscured by a looped peasant hood, tried to get by Zhivana the same way. She engaged him, forcing him back with her greater reach. Behind her she heard a male voice cry out in pain and then Par cursing. She didn't spare a glance, however, focusing on her own opponent.

"Considerable Crimes Division," she managed to get out between calculated thrusts. She didn't want to kill him; it was tough to question dead people. "Stop. Fighting."

"Surrender," Par said, coming up beside her with his own sword out.

Zhivana danced to the side around an overturned chair. They had the big man backed up almost to the wall.

"Git you crows to Annunaki," the man growled. He glanced over his shoulder and Zhivana started to cry a warning.

The man threw his knife at Par and sprang backward, crashing through the thin windowpane. *He can't get away, not on my first case.* Zhivana dropped her sword and jumped after him, claws extending as she caught his waist. Wrapped together, they fell toward the stone street below, landing with a sickening crunch that jarred Zhivana all the way to the tips of her ears.

CHAPTER FOUR

"You two are supposed to be solving a murder, not creating more bodies." Hajjar had come down to the scene himself, which Zhivana guessed was not a good sign. Behind him the medical assistants were loading the unfortunate thug into a cart, his head twisted at a horrible angle.

"It's only one body," Par pointed out. "Zhivana's unhurt, how was she supposed to know she'd fall with him under? Not like we were high up." He motioned to the shattered window above.

Zhivana ducked away from the medical apprentice trying to check her for wounds and looked at Par in surprise. She hadn't expected him to defend her actions. *Definitely need to give him more of a chance*, she decided.

"The other one left a blood trail," she said. "Any chance we can get a sniffer team out to track?" She'd worked with the sniffers before, tracking thieves and missing persons across the city, but wasn't sure on the CCD procedure.

"Already on their way." Hajjar turned to her. "You've blood on your sleeve, are you hurt?"

"It's his, I think," Zhivana said, not meeting the Lieutenant's dark gaze. The last thing she needed was someone checking for a wound that wouldn't be there anymore. "I apologize about that; him, I mean. I didn't want him to get away."

"You going to need time?" Par asked. His tone was slightly scornful but his eyes showed the bluff as they crinkled in what she could have sworn was either compassion or repressed mirth.

"She's killed before," Hajjar said in a flat tone.

"I'm fine." Zhivana glanced between them, wondering what the history there was. Tension she couldn't read radiated between the two men.

One of the Watch officers who'd responded to the runner she and Par had sent to the nearest station walked over. "Here's his identification," he said, oblivious to the subtext happening around them.

"He had his tags on him? While committing a crime?" Par shook his head.

"Well, sure," Zhivana said as she took the thin, engraved copper disk. She smiled at the Watch officer, vaguely recognizing the young, fair-haired human. He served with Kitnemovich's division, she thought. "You have to carry your tags, no matter what."

"The law says so, but the law also says not to break into people's homes and tear apart their things." Par snorted.

"Greenies got none besty than tip a 'nocent a muzzler over they tags," Zhivana said, dropping her voice into the sing-song of the slums.

Par laughed outright and even Hajjar's stern face cracked in a faint smile. The officer just stared.

"Not from around here, eh?" she said.

"No, Cordonate." He bit his lip. "I just transferred in from the Militia. Only been in the city half a year."

"Might do you good to spend a little time down in the Docks or out in Cliffside. Take friends and no currency bigger than a seed. Got to learn the people if you're going to police them." She clapped him on the shoulder, part of her wishing she were still Watch, could take this new boy under her wing and show him the ropes in good old Watch tradition.

"*Sow's Ear* is a good place to sit and listen," Par added, surprising Zhivana once again.

A large, caged-in cart arrived, the old grey draft mare pulling up just outside the alley they stood in. A kirgani woman climbed down from beside the driver. She wore the green and russet of the Watch, but with a large silver patch in the shape of a cat sewn over her left breast. The sniffer had arrived.

The young officer retreated with a blush and a muttered thank you. Hajjar folded his long arms across his chest and inclined his head toward the new arrivals.

"You two can take it from here. Try not to kill anyone else. I'll go round up a clerk to start the paperwork for you. When you're done here, come back to Division." He didn't wait for more than a nod of acknowledgment from either of them before striding out of the alley and disappearing around the side of the rickety wood and stone buildings.

"Yes, Zir," Zhivana said to his retreating back. She glanced at Par who shrugged and they both walked up to where the sniffer was unlatching the gate on the cage.

The deep lion leapt out on command and sat calmly with its eyeless, snow-pure head tipped comically to one side while the keeper clipped a lead to the thick leather collar. Zhivana shivered, the musky smell of the deep lion awakening something primal in her blood. The creature's head came up nearly to her waist and its long feline body would stretch over their heads if it stood on its back legs. The cat stretched and licked at the air. Deep lions were blind, totally eyeless but with thick nose pads and large, agile ears. In the spring sunlight his short-haired coat was a translucent white, but in the dark it would phosphoresce. They could track almost anything for miles, even in the crowded city.

"Hello, Amurshaya," Par said softly to the deep lion, moving up beside Zhivana.

"Zi Nedragovna," the kirgani sniffer said. She looked familiar, standing taller than Zhivana, with a deep brown coat and bold black striping over her neck and between her ears.

"Zi Pravovna," Zhivana said, offering a hand as she recalled the woman's name. "How's Oblev?" Her mate was a friend of Zhivana's own and they worked together on commissions from time to time. She'd met the sniffer only once before and was pleased she'd recalled the name.

"He's well," Pravovna answered even as Par said, "You know each other?"

"Sure, don't all kirgani band together?" Zhivana shook her head.

"Funny."

"If you two are done sniping, I've got a trail to follow?" Pravovna looked between them and her ears twitched as though to say "not my problem."

Par showed her where the trail began and the deep lion followed Pravovna's spoken commands, sniffing at the blood before yanking her off down the street. Cries of surprise and wonder followed them as they pushed through the small crowd of bystanders. Zhivana perched on the rickety steps to watch the sniffer as the team headed off down Scill Crossing, turned into another winding alley, and disappeared from her sight.

"So who's our thug?" Par asked as they entered the cramped apartment for the second time.

Zhivana checked the tag she still held. "Ampor Gouri; we'll have to check for an address." She said it without much hope. No one at the records office ever checked the addresses given as long as the citizen could offer proof of birth in Pyrrh or had family members vouching for them, and criminal types rarely listed real addresses.

"Probably lives in the middle of one of the bridges, if it's anything like half the addresses listed with tags in this city," Par muttered, echoing her thoughts. "I'll sic one of our clerks on the name and face. We can get a sketch done of that ugly bastard that ran, if Amurshaya and his keeper can't track him down."

"You spend a lot of time with the sniffers?" Zhivana glanced at him as they stood in the doorway and surveyed the trashed room.

"I like cats," Par said with a shrug. "I wonder how this place looked before they got to it."

"From the smell? Not too different." She nudged a broken chair with her boot. The room didn't stink, exactly, but it had an under-taste of fruit left in the sun too long and dirt not often swept up.

"What were they looking for?" Par walked over to the packed trunk and flipped up the catch. The contents were neatly folded and entirely undisturbed.

"Could be coincidence." She spread her arms as Par gave her his don't be stupid look again. "Clearly our nesting pair weren't moving in here. Dodgy area, tiny rooms, bad decorating."

"Clothing, a notebook." Par dug through the trunk. "Looks like alchemy stuff," he said as he flipped through the book's thick pages.

Zhivana moved to the hearth, rolling her torn and bloody sleeve up so that it wouldn't look quite so conspicuous. The hearth doubled as a kitchen area, and she found the source of the smell in a covered basket of overripe glenmelons, the green and purple flesh turning slowly black. There was an iron pot that had a rim of starchy grains stuck inside. The sideboard was empty when Zhivana slid the doors aside. If the victim had owned dishes or table settings, there were none evident.

"This doesn't add up at all. There's nothing to steal here, except possibly these bronze candlesticks and maybe the alchemy notes, though we'd have to check to see if they're anything important and I don't see how a thief would know anyway." Par banged the candlesticks together as he shoved them back into the pile in the trunk. "This is getting us nowhere."

"Heyla, go easy on that," she said as he kicked the trunk hard enough that it screeched and slid over the bare pine floor. "You've got a point," Zhivana added as he glared at her and looked ready to storm out of the building. "We've got a pregnant lover all ready to go somewhere and lying about it, a hard to locate and possible-addict mother, a victim who works a soft job in the Treasury, just got promoted, and yet seems to be living in near-poverty, and two thieves who break in for apparently no reason and trash the place while ignoring the one thing in the room that might hold something valuable."

"And were willing to fight to the death instead of being taken in." Par took the alchemy book and slammed the trunk lid shut.

In all her years in the Watch, Zhivana had seen many people willing to fight and die for seemingly stupid reasons. But usually it came down to one thing. Fear. Fear of the fines, fear of the mines, fear of the executioner. "We need to find the smashed face one. Someone hired them. If they didn't want to get taken in, they either have a record or they don't want someone to think they're talking to the Law."

"Time to go do the exciting part of the job," Par said. "Paperwork."

A Division artist caught them at the doorway to the Graveshift office and they detoured to a room on the second floor so the slim, nervous young woman could do a rough sketch and take down a description of the sword-wielding thief who'd fled their victim's apartment. She worked efficiently with a graphite stick, making small changes as they recalled details until she had a sketch and description that both Par and Zhivana could agree looked like the fugitive.

By the time they were done, word had come in from the Sniffer that her deep lion had lost the scent in the network of canals that started in the Four Bridges. Most likely he'd either had a boat waiting for him or stolen one and gotten away by water. No one swam in the fetid green-grey water unless they were truly desperate.

"Pity no one noticed a bleeding man taking a boat," Par muttered.

"In this city?" Zhivana shrugged and turned to the artist who was cleaning up her drawing. "Can you get this out before shift change? And to the Docks and Old Town first."

"Sure, Zira. I'll take it straight to the printers. Any instructions you want added for the Watch?" Her voice was steadier than her eyes and Zhivana wondered if the girl was on Fell Dust or perhaps opiates, or if she was just naturally weird.

"Just the usual. Have him brought in, notify that he's armed, injured, and dangerous," Par answered as Zhivana glanced his way, unsure of protocol for the CCD.

They were almost back up the steps again when another messenger came looking for them, and with a sigh they both turned around and headed down to the Victim Morgue.

"He died from multiple stab wounds to the body. Technically, it was the blood loss that killed him." Narumi Kido, the CCD Master Medical Examiner, winked at Par and Zhivana.

Zhivana wasn't sure she'd ever seen an anuran wink before and found the glide of the double lids somewhat disturbing as the second eyelid closed from side to side instead of up and down. Usually when they blinked, they only blinked the outer lids.

"Great, Kido, so glad we took all those stairs down here to confirm what our own eyes already told us." Par grimaced at the naked body on the stone slab.

Akil Gerges looked more dead, vulnerable, and sad then he had lying on the street. His wounds, washed clean, gaped like hungry mouths, bone showing in places. Zhivana, breathing through her clenched teeth, mentally sent a prayer to the Shadow Lord for his spirit, though she guessed Akil himself would probably have prayed to Enlil or Anunnaki. The CCD autopsy chamber was clean and smelled more of water and chemicals than death, but the sickly sweet stench of old blood had permeated the stones and seemed to seep into Zhivana's fur the longer she stood here.

"What kind of weapon are we looking for?" Zhivana asked, resisting the temptation to elbow Par or just flee this place of death and sadness. She doubted anybody ended up here after a natural death.

"Dagger, with the tip missing. It broke off in his breastbone. I've got the piece here for you. I'd guess a blade around a handsbreadth given the depth of some of these wounds. If you find me the right dagger I can match the break most likely." She pointed to a dish that held a bright gold sun coin in it. "That's why I called you down though, not the wounds."

"A sun? That wasn't on the body." Par picked up the coin and turned it. The surface glinted silver and then gold as he flipped it around beneath the bright lights. Apparently the medical wing of CCD had the budget for alchemist lamps.

"Nope." Kido's smile was very wide, revealing her double rows of tiny, flat, black teeth, like a mouth full of obsidian. "It was *in* the body."

Par dropped the coin with a curse and Zhivana chuckled right along with Kido. This anuran wasn't half bad, she decided; maybe the job wouldn't turn out to be so bad, either. At least there was someone around with a sense of humor who wasn't afraid of Par's constantly angry demeanor.

"Careful with that," Kido said. "Not every day that I get a handsome tip from one of my customers."

"It's evidence. Where in the corpse was it?" Par asked, glaring at them both, but saving the longer glare for his partner.

"Throat. He swallowed it, but it hadn't time to reach his belly. Must have been just before he died." Kido stopped chuckling as she answered.

"Any sign it was forced into his mouth?" Zhivana leaned over the corpse, still breathing through her teeth. She couldn't tell much, but he didn't seem to have chipped teeth or any obvious sign of trauma.

"Not that I can tell. Not conclusively. But he could have swallowed it under duress. A knife in the back can be pretty persuasive." The ME shrugged her bony shoulders, her fine grey-green scales rippling along the exposed skin of her neck.

"What are you thinking?" Par looked at Zhivana as she paced away from the body, crossing to the end of the long, cold room.

"Could be a money-owed situation. A message." Zhivana turned back as she reached the wall. She'd seen things like this before; bodies left with a particular carved mark in their skin or a significant object. Usually a warning to family or people who owed money. But something about this situation bothered her. "A sun though? That's an expensive message. That coin looks brand new. I bet he paid less than a sun in rent on that dump of his."

"Must be a serious debt," Par said. He turned back to Kido, who watched the two of them with interest. "You do any tests on his blood yet? Could he have been on something?"

"Not a lot of blood left in him to test, but no marks in the usual places and no scarring in his nasal passages or throat. I wasn't going to open him up fully since we know the cause of death, but I can do it and look at his organs if you think it's necessary."

"No, that's all right." Par sighed. "His lover will be down to identify him, so maybe cover him up? And keep her here until we get to talk to her, if you would."

"Sure, green-eyes." Kido smiled softly at him and gently rested her hand on his arm for a moment. Zhivana watched an unspoken message pass between them and wondered at the compassion on the ME's broad face.

She knew Par had lost his partner during a bust gone very wrong, Cordonate Kalja Tawwab's death had been all over the daily sheets and talked about in hushed whispers in the taverns and on patrol late at night. But that had been months ago. She figured he'd be past it, at least ready to be assigned someone new. But maybe Hajjar had made that decision without Par's complete acquiescence. It would certainly go far to explain the tension between them earlier. Watching the ME's gentle face, Zhivana wondered suddenly if there hadn't been more between Par and the dead woman than publically known.

She shrugged it off. None of her business, so long as he did his job. Wasn't like he was keen to share his private feelings anyway. *More likely to rip my head off than cry on my shoulder.*

"Good," Par muttered, turning away with suspiciously bright eyes. "Back upstairs?"

CHAPTER FIVE

A runner arrived from the printer with copies of the artist's sketch of their unknown thief. Par pinned one to the board assigned to the Gerges case and stepped away. The case board had pathetically little on it. A handful of names and one sketch. No one had much motive to kill this guy, not that Par could see. If it had been retribution for a debt, why kill the person in the family most likely to be able to pay it back?

"If he owed money, why kill him? Why so many wounds? If it wasn't for a debt, why the sun down his throat?" Zhivana voiced his thoughts as she paced in front of the board.

Par found her quick movements annoying and glared pointedly at one of the chairs. She ignored him.

"What'd the lover say?" Keen leaned against a desk, watching Zhivana with fascination.

Par shook his head. Hajjar should have assigned her to Keen and Mikal, even if that left him partnerless. Especially if it left him partnerless.

"Not much," Zhivana said. "She lied about moving in with Akil, unless they had a third place they were going. But I doubt she crept out of her home in the middle of the night, walked to Old Town, stabbed her lover beneath a streetlamp, and then waddled home in time to put on that show for us this morning." Zhivana mercifully stopped pacing, and stood, staring at the board.

"She seemed genuinely distraught. We could always bug her when she comes in, see if the beetles detect her lying." Par shrugged.

Mikal shook his head. "They don't accurately react with already high emotion though."

Par sighed. Mikal had a point. The truth beetles did a fair job of reacting to changes in heart rate and minute signs of deception, but on an already upset person they'd probably react anyway. He was sure the widow was lying about something, but he had nothing to go on other than a sketch and a coin. His fists tightened and he winced as his nails dug into his palms. *Focus on the job, solve your case. Nothing to be angry about. Just get through the day.*

"Then we let the sketch circulate and hope something pops until we can talk to the widow." He turned away from the board. "Time to finish up some reports, I guess."

Zhivana shrugged. "Where's my desk?" she asked.

Par motioned, but stopped short as Kamilah and her partner Hashim came laughing through the doorway.

"Heyla, Par." Kamilah's rich voice filled the room. "You're his new partner, eh?" She smiled at the kirgani.

"Zhivana Nedragovna, meet Kamilah Bazzi and Hashim Morcos." Par made the introductions, watching Zhivana closely. He was tense, ready to cut her off if she said anything about Kamilah's appearance.

The Cordonate had been beyond beautiful before a jealous lover had drugged her and taken a blade to her. Deep scars cut across her nose and warped her full mouth and a crescent of pale scar tissue marred the line of her jaw. From what Par had heard, her body looked nearly as patchwork. Kamilah wore her hair long and loose, the thick black waves falling over the worst of the scarring and softening the effects.

Zhivana stepped forward with a smile and nodded politely, offering her hand in greeting. "Good to see you again, zi Bazzi," she said.

"Kamilah," she said, returning the smile as she clasped hands. "We're all on the same level now. No reason for formalities."

Par let out his breath slowly and looked between them. "You already know each other?"

"Zhivana helped me and my former partner track down a summoner... , what? Five years back?" Kamilah shrugged.

"Six," Zhivana said. A shadow of dark emotion flickered through her oceanic eyes, but was gone so quickly Par wondered if he'd imagined it.

"I'm her new partner," Hashim said, the slender man stepping forward to clasp hands with her as well. "Alilim retired a couple years ago."

"You two catch a case this morning as well?" Par asked.

"Nah, we were down at the High Courts. Had to meet with one of the Justicars about the Hydriani case. It's finally going forward, though one of our witnesses is shaky at best." Hashim nodded at the case board behind Par. "Looks like you guys caught something?"

"Murder in Old Town," Zhivana said.

"Stop the presses!" Kamilah laughed. "Mugging gone wrong? Or some two-bit roll her customer?"

"Neither, so far as we can tell. Looks like a debt thing, maybe. Found a new-minted sun in his throat and a couple of thugs tossing his place." Par waved at the sketch of the smashed-nose thug.

"Wait a minute," Kamilah stepped up to the board and cocked her head to one side. "Gerges. That sounds familiar."

"In court today," Hashim said. "Wasn't that crazy old bird who tried to throw her shoe at the scheduling judge named Gerges?"

"Nansilla Gerges? She's the victim's mother." Par felt renewed excitement shiver through him. Maybe they weren't totally stalled-out yet. Anything to save him from paperwork, from a quiet afternoon without action to distract him from memories of Kalja, from having to look up and see a stranger sitting at her desk.

"I don't remember her full name, sorry." Hashim glanced at Kamilah as she turned back to them. She shook her head.

"Crazy, though. Detoxing I guess. She was in for arraignment. We sat in session while waiting on Justicar Majid."

"She still in holding?" Par dared to hope.

"Don't think so. Released. But she has a court date sometime next week if I remember what was said well enough. Her counsel would know more," Hashim said.

"Do you know her counsel's name?" Par asked. She'd been booked at the courts, so someone would have a record. But it'd take less time if they didn't have to track down the keeper of that paperwork, especially since the paperwork would be fresh and so might be in transit.

"We might recall, yes." Kamilah shrugged, her unscarred eyebrow raised as she tortured Par a little. She was fully aware that giving him the information would spare him and Zhivana a hunt through the High Courts' notorious bureaucracy.

"And her counsel would be?" Zhivana didn't give Kamilah any time to hold her knowledge over Par's head.

He glanced at his partner and pressed his mouth into a line. Kamilah's little games were just her way of caring.

Kamilah held her arms up in surrender. "No patience at all." She laughed again. "An anuran, name's Haru Tojo. He probably has more cases this afternoon, so you'd better get going to catch him before second session starts."

"Good luck," Hashim called after them as Par grabbed his jacket and he and Zhivana headed out the door with barely a glance spared between them.

They caught up to Haru Tojo just as he was leaving his third floor office at the High Court building. They'd sprinted over to the huge complex from CCD and Par was still panting, Zhivana noticed. She tried not to feel smug that she'd easily out-paced him and was still breathing normally.

The anuran Counsel was short for his race, barely coming above Zhivana's waist. His fine scales were patterned pale brown and soft purple, and his suit was tastefully colored to match in cream linen and lavender wool. He looked annoyed as they came to a halt outside his open office door, waving their badges at the busy clerk out front.

"Counsel Tojo?" Par asked, even though the door had a plaque that identified him.

"I'm due in court soon with a long list of deserving clients, Cordonate. What do you want?" The Counsel inclined his head a fraction but didn't stop buttoning his vest or even really look at them as he turned to gather papers.

"*Okaeri,* Counsel," Zhivana said, stepping in past Par. Her partner's lack of tact would not go over well with the socially careful anura. She wondered that anyone talked to Par at all given his abrupt and abrasive ways. Maybe she'd caught him on a bad day. *Or maybe it's me.*

"*Okaeri ista,*" Tojo responded, his golden eyes widening in surprise at the formal greeting.

"We won't take much of your time," Zhivana said, pulling out her notebook and inkstone nub. "We're looking for a woman named Nansilla Gerges and heard she might be assigned to you?"

"For what do you need her?" Tojo sighed. "She a suspect?"

"Her son was killed early this morning," Par said. His breathing had evened out and he folded his arms, stepping up beside Zhivana. "We don't think she's a suspect, but haven't had a chance to talk to her."

"She was in a Watch holding cell since yesterday evening, so I'd say she has a solid alibi," Tojo said. "But I have an address, which is what I suppose you want. You may get it from my clerk. If you decide to arrest her, I'd appreciate notification before you hand her to a Justicar. It'll save me some paperwork."

"Thank you, Counsel," Zhivana murmured. "*Ja ne.*"

"*Ja ne,* Cordonate." Tojo picked up his paper and nodded to Zhivana. He told his clerk to give them zira Gerges's address on the way out.

"Back to Old Town," Par muttered. He turned to Zhivana as they left the High Courts and headed for the CCD stables. "Where'd you learn anuran?"

"I didn't, not really," she said. His considering expression amused her. Maybe now he'd finally decide to see what she could do before he wrote her off. "I know a few words, the formal greeting and farewell, that sort of thing. And only the city dialect."

"Came in handy," Par said and shrugged, looking uncomfortable.

Zhivana watched him stride past her and let him lead the way to find Faris. A few hours ago she'd pegged him for a typical close-minded, human bigot. Gods knew there were plenty of anti-anuran and anti-kirgani people in the city despite the official policy of inclusion and diversity. The anuran got less of the hate since they were numerous in Pyrrh and they held some high offices in the Guilds. She guessed that was an advantage to being native to the islands and swamps all along the coast. While the humans outnumbered either of the other races, the anuran outnumbered the kirgani population at least three to one.

And no one liked immigrants, human or otherwise. A hundred years of relative peace hadn't acclimated the humans to their furry neighbors yet, it seemed.

It didn't hurt, in Zhivana's mind at least, that the anuran resembled humans more than her people did. Scales and double-lidded eyes aside, their features were still basically human. She'd even heard of anuran-human matings, though no children had ever come of one. She was pretty damn sure no human would ever consider trying to mate with a kirgani. Of course, she wasn't sure why any kirgani would want a human. No fur and they smelled a bit... off. With a sigh she lengthened her stride and moved to catch up with her partner. She'd definitely try to give him more of a chance. If only he'd give her one.

Nansilla Gerges was a woman aged by drugs and hard living. Her stringy, light brown hair was pulled back into a greasy knot at the nape of her neck, and she stared suspiciously at Par and Zhivana with yellowed eyes, refusing to open the bare plank door more than a hand's breadth.

"I just got me carting date. I didn't do nothing 'cept come home," her words slurred as she spoke, her skin breaking out in a sweat.

Zhivana found herself breathing through her mouth for at least the third time that day. Zi Gerges' building was a converted inn, the rooms let out for very little to those scraping by on whatever they could, populated by a variety of petty criminals and addicts commonly haunting the alleys of Old Town. The smell of raw liquor and poppy smoke permeated the rough wooden walls and drifted out from under warped doors.

"We want to talk to you about your son," Par said. He sounded as though his own teeth were gritted, though from the smell or from his lack of patience, Zhivana couldn't tell. Probably both.

"My son?" Nansilla opened the door a little wider and her expression shifted from suspicious to confused. "Akil's not here. He don't come around."

"Zira, please, let us in. This is not a conversation for a hallway." Zhivana stepped up beside her partner.

The woman's rheumy eyes widened and she mutely nodded, stepping back.

The single room apartment was far worse than her son's had been. The bed was a straw-stuffed mattress against one wall. The only heat was a small bronze brazier full of smoldering coal in the middle of a room that cried out 'fire hazard'. The tiny window had no glass, just a shutter which was cracked open to allow the smoke to vent. The smell of vermin, vomit, and poppy smoke threatened to overpower Zhivana, and she barely resisted gagging. She could almost hear the fleas and gods knew what else crawling through the piles of dirty clothing and bedding.

"You always take me to the nicest places," she muttered under her breath as she stepped in close to Par's shoulder.

He snorted, clearly having heard her. "You may want to sit down, zi Gerges," he said. If the filth was getting to him as badly as it was to Zhivana, he gave no sign beyond the tightening of his jaw. Sometimes, she guessed, dull human senses were a blessing.

Their victim's mother looked around her as though lost and then sank down onto the bed, her eyes flicking nervously to the one piece of furniture, a large wardrobe with stylized trees carved into its double door. Zhivana was willing to bet a seed or two that her poppy stash was in there somewhere. She forced her hackles to lay flat and shook out her hands a little as she and Par stepped further into the room. She wasn't a Watch officer anymore, busting people over drugs wasn't part of her job. Besides, the woman had just lost a son and already had a court date. This was no time to be a zealot.

Par cleared his throat and she realized they were both staring at her. *Thanks, partner*, she thought. She had no illusions that he was leaving this task to her because he respected her manner or was particularly worried about his own.

"Zira," Zhivana began, wondering how many times today she'd have to say these words. "Akil is dead."

"Dead?" She looked as though the word held no meaning. "He's not dead. You take me for a cloud buyer? What do you crows really want?"

She ignored the slur. "Well, zira, you can come back with us to Division and we'll let you identify the body yourself. But I don't think there's been a mistake." Zhivana shifted from one foot to the other, hoping that the woman would agree to come with them. She'd far rather conduct an interview in the relative cleanliness of Division than here.

Par had the apprentice medallion half out of his belt, but he slipped it back in. Apparently he, too, wanted the woman to come with them.

"You've made a mistake," Nansilla said, getting to her feet with effort. "We'll see about this." She hesitated as they turned toward the door. "You aren't tricking me? Puffing this to get me go quiet?" she asked, focusing her suspicious gaze on Zhivana.

"No, zira. No tricks. We aren't here to bust your muzzle or shake you down." She sighed. Figured, heaping the distrust on the kirgani instead of her human partner. But Par was at least being quiet, which was probably as close as he got to civil.

"You'd better bring me home, and apologize what for giving me chest pains, once it's clear you've made a terrible mistake." With a self-righteous shake of her hunched shoulders, Nansilla led them out of her room and locked the door behind her.

"Killers! Derricks!" Nansilla didn't look so small and old with her jaundiced eyes glowing in fury and her hands curved like talons as she flew at Zhivana.

Zhivana and Parshan wrestled the distraught woman to the floor as gently as they could while Kido quickly drew the sheet up over the corpse. Par murmured soothing things under his breath and surprised Zhivana again with his sudden compassion toward the raving, struggling mother. She grit her teeth and held on until Nansilla's sobs subsided and she lay heaving underneath them on the damp stones.

"How," Nansilla whispered after a moment. "Who did this to him? Was it that rank hussy? I'll…" she broke down into sobs again.

Zhivana glanced at Par. His moss-green eyes glinted with some emotion she couldn't read and for the first time since she'd met him he truly seemed present and not a thread away from murder. He nodded and they let the woman up, helping her to stand.

"We need to talk to you, zira. Come with me. We'll get you some tea." Par tucked her arm beneath his and led her out as though escorting royalty.

Zhivana shook her head. His moods were going to drive her crazy. Crazier, anyway.

"He's still adjusting," Kido said, coming up beside her. Zhivana started, not used to forgetting someone was in the room.

"He's… volatile." She looked at the ME and spread her hands. "Is every day here this exciting?" She was thinking of the morning and her abrupt introduction to her partner. Zhivana wondered if they tossed every new Cordonate into the deep like this.

"He's grieving. In some ways, we all are. She was Hajjar's niece, you know." Kido rolled her bony shoulders, but her golden eyes stayed fixed on Zhivana.

His niece? That did explain some things, though she guessed there was still a damnable lot unsaid about Parshan and his former partner. She opened her mouth to ask but stopped herself. This wasn't the time, and for all she liked the ME, they weren't known to each other, not really. She wasn't planning on quitting just because of one annoying day. There'd be time to figure out the subtext in the future.

"I didn't know," she said instead. "I'd better go. *Ja ne*, thank you."

Kido blinked with all four lids, slowly, and then smiled. "*Ja ne*. You'll do." She patted Zhivana awkwardly on her back and then turned to her work, shuffling instruments on a tray in clear dismissal.

Upstairs in one of the sparsely-furnished questioning rooms, Par raised an eyebrow at her but otherwise didn't question how far behind him she'd fallen. Qays ducked into the room with a mug of steaming tea which he set in front of the blank-faced zi Gerges. The tea cut the smell of urine and stale poppies that seemed to fill the room the longer the grieving mother sat there. Par and Zhivana took the two stools across the narrow table and waited for a little while.

Par already had a copy of the drawing of the broken-nosed thief resting on the narrow table beneath his hand. He slid it across to Akil's mother. "Recognize him at all?"

"This the man what killed my boy?" Nansilla said after a moment of staring at the picture and then shaking her head. Her face had betrayed no recognition, just sorrow with anger smoldering beneath.

"We don't know, zira." Par pulled the drawing away.

Nansilla sniffled into her tea, rocking back and forth in the chair and refusing to meet their eyes. Par sat back and said nothing, watching Zhivana out of the corner of his eye.

"Did your son owe anyone money?" Zhivana finally said, pulling out her notebook. She felt as rude as Par usually was, but they needed information and there was no bloody time to wait for her to get over her son's death. Or even sober up.

"No," she said. Impotent rage put life back into her jaundiced eyes and she glared, desperately needing a vent for it. Nansilla's tone implied Zhivana was a bitch for even asking, and once again Zhivana was forced to smooth her hackles and take a calming breath. The woman wasn't really blaming her, after all.

"Did you?" Par said gently, leaning forward to catch Nansilla's attention.

Her chin came up and Zhivana noticed a particularly prominent mole on her wrinkled throat. "No. Well, not lately," she amended. "My boy gives me 'nough bits to live on, though *she* don't like it."

"Jala? She said you didn't approve of them moving in together." Par seemed comfortable taking the lead now and Zhivana sighed. She realized she might as well give up trying to predict what her partner would do and just play along. She detested the awkwardness of it, like trying to cram herself into a badly-tailored shirt.

Nansilla's expression turned hard though her voice trembled as she spoke. "Did she murder my baby?"

"No, zira, not that we can figure. She's heavily pregnant and he was killed on the street in the middle of the night, not in their home."

"Do you know why he kept a separate residence? Where they were moving to?" Zhivana couldn't help but cut in.

"Moving? Why would they move? Where did she say they were going?" Her jaundiced eyes narrowed, and when she pursed her lips they turned from a worn mouth to a network of fine creases.

Interesting. So Jala had definitely been lying. It wasn't too surprising that Akil wouldn't have told his mother about a move, but something tickled the back of Zhivana's mind, nagging at her. Moving. But maybe not within the city? She thrust the itchy thought away and concentrated on the mother.

"Who might have been owed money, or held a grudge against your son?" Par was saying as Zhivana drew her attention back to the interview, making a note on her pad.

"Please, zi Gerges, it'll help us immensely," she added as the woman looked guiltily down into her half empty mug.

"Mukmed, they call him 'Knucklebones'," she said softly. "But he ain't stomped around me for weeks now, so I figured Akil paid him down."

Zhivana sucked in her breath. She knew all about Knucklebones. He was one of the raggy sharks, what the scrubber class called the petty crime bosses who ran the underbelly of the slum districts: Cliffside, the Levi, the Docks, and Old Town. He'd gotten his moniker — so the stories said — from the knucklebones of his enemies which hung from a golden chain around his neck.

Par raised an eyebrow at her and she nodded.

"He's the type to have his fingers in everything and still keep his hands clean. The Watch hasn't ever pinned anything that stuck," she muttered. "What's he look like?" she asked in a louder voice.

"Bald, about as tall as him but with more pork to him." Nansilla nodded at Par and then closed her eyes. "Fond o' wearing red."

"Address?" Par asked. It was a lead.

"He takes business at the *Roost Lay*." Nansilla didn't open her eyes and a heavy tear tore free, running down her cheek. Slowly others followed, the tracks blending in clean streaks down her face.

"We'll have a carriage ready for you, just ask the clerk and they'll take you home. Stick around town, though, we might have more questions." Par rose.

"I don't have the bits to afford his burning," she whispered.

"There's a fund for murder victims. I'll see a clerk gets you paperwork for that," Par said and again Zhivana was surprised by his gentleness.

Outside the room, Zhivana caught Par's arm. His muscles were tensed like cables beneath her hand and she winced as he jerked away from her, turning to give her a flat look.

"We should get some officers to come with us," she said. "I've heard of him; Knucklebones won't likely come without a fight, if we can get near him at all."

Par grinned at her, and the now-familiar angry burn kindled in his eyes. "Good. I feel like punching something. Repeatedly."

Zhivana thought of the hollow-eyed, guilty mother, and couldn't disagree with that. Without a word she shrugged and followed him out.

CHAPTER SIX

The *Roost Lay* was an ancient wood and brick building on the cliff side of Old Town. Nominally it was a pushing school, a place for fencers to duel and practice; the upstairs rented by the hour to un-licensed whores not wanting to pay their dues to the Carnal Guild. In the middle of the afternoon there were a few loiterers around, but the streets were mostly bare in this area since the usual crowd of bored students and tired dockworkers wouldn't get going until evening. As they drove up, Zhivana glanced around, noting the place was less than a double handful of streets from their murder scene.

Par had Faris stop and let them out down the pitted road from the school. Zhivana studied the street for a moment and then caught Par's arm as he tried to go forward.

"There's a back entrance to that place, guaranteed. We walk in the front; they'll be gone before we make it through."

"So go around back," Par said, glaring at her hand on his arm.

"Faris," Zhivana said, turning away from her frustrating partner. "There's a Watch booth over on Karrim road. Notify them we need a couple bodies, will you?"

"Sure thing, Cordonate," the quiet driver said. He clucked to his horse and wheeled away, turning the light cart expertly on the uneven cobbles.

"You really like your backup, don't you?" Par muttered. He followed her under the eaves of a townhome.

"Maybe I just don't like the idea of my partner getting killed on my first day." She responded more testily than she'd meant.

He flinched and his upper lip curled into a snarl. He looked like he might say something, but instead he jerked around to look down the street. After a long, tense moment, Zhivana could hear him counting under his breath.

"This place is rather near our crime scene," Zhivana pointed out, not sure how she'd pissed him off this time. He shrugged, but didn't face her or stop muttering numbers.

"That's enough," he said after a count just above a hundred. "They'll be along soon with Faris. Let's go."

"Damnit, Par," she started to say, but he was already moving away. If their quarry escaped out the back, so be it. They'd just have to run or call in the sniffers again. With the sea cliffs so close her keen ears could pick up the thunder of wave on rock, at least the directions Knucklebones could run in were limited.

She couldn't let Par go in alone. He'd either kill someone or end up dead, judging from his tense expression. Zhivana lengthened her stride to catch up, though she couldn't resist a snide remark about his knowledge of numbers that she was sure he heard.

The front door was open, letting the spring breeze into the long front room. A stairway was cut into one of the short walls, leading up to the second floor. Low-quality practice foils were hung neatly in racks along one wall and two foppishly dressed men reclined on a couch next to a door in the back of the room. They passed a bottle of wine between them and grinned lewdly at Par and Zhivana.

Zhivana approached them carefully, her eyes darting around the dim interior, her ears flicking as she heard the muted sounds of movement on the floor above. Par, she noticed, had his hand resting lightly on his short sword.

"Crows are out early," one of the dandies remarked as he wiped his sleeve over his lips.

"Caw, caw," the other said, too loudly. "Are you here as dispatch or derrick?"

Zhivana's ears picked up a scuffling movement on the other side of the door and someone calling out "crows!"

"Go," she hissed at Par. "They've called warning. Go through."

He grabbed the door and wrenched it open even as he dragged his sword free of the sheath. "You?" he asked, hesitating.

"I'm going over, meet you around back," she called, sprinting for the stairs. There was always the possibility Knucklebones would head for the roof instead. *Should've waited for the Watch.*

She took the stairs two and three at a time, coming to a landing in a dim hallway. She sprinted down the length, nearly bowling over a sleepy human woman who leaned out of a door while pulling a robe over her naked breasts. There was another stairway at the back, going down to where she heard shouting and a commotion. It also went up steeply to a latched hatch she guessed led to the roof.

No time for hesitation. Zhivana went up, deciding she'd get a better view of the street and surrounds from there. The roof wasn't entirely flat but sloped gently to the back. She ran to the edge, leaning her weight into the slope to keep from sliding on the wet tiles. A squat man in a gaudy red jacket paused in the alley below and glanced toward the back door. Par's voice yelling obscenities somewhere below her brought a grim smile to her face. Nobody had killed him, at least.

Red jacket. Bald. Fat. The man now slipping down the alley seemed to fit the description. Zhivana leapt off the roof and rolled into the fall as she landed, ignoring a searing pain in her hip.

Baldy noticed her flying leap and took off at a pathetic run that was more of a waddling hop. She followed, reaching for her hand crossbow. It wasn't in her belt. *Wormshit. Must have fallen out when I rolled.* She drew her sword instead.

"CCD," she yelled, putting on enough speed to catch up to the man.

He stopped running and spun, pulling a long knife from beneath his flapping jacket. "Back off, bitch."

"No," she growled. "You back off. I've already killed someone today and doing two reports instead of one won't take me longer. Give me an excuse, pug pincher."

For a moment it looked like he would. Then his eyes flicked beyond her and she heard Par calling her name. Knucklebones straightened up out of his fighting crouch and dropped the knife. "I ain't done nothing. You wanna waste city salaries, be my pleasure."

Zhivana reached with one hand for her cinch cuffs and found that she'd forgotten yet another thing. She didn't remember putting them on her belt that morning. Not the brightest first day in history, that was for sure. She felt like over a decade of experience had flown right out, leaving her a stumbling rookie again.

"Parshan!" she yelled. "Down this way, I need your cinch."

Pounding footsteps echoed off the buildings but she didn't turn though her back itched and her hackles stiffened. She didn't dare take her eyes off the man in front of her. She'd be a rookie in truth to believe he had only the one knife on him.

"I got him," Par said, moving past her and kicking the knife away from Knucklebones. He gripped the bigger man's arms and flipped him around with relative ease. Zhivana sheathed her sword after a glance behind her revealed two uniformed Watch officers, one a sergeant judging from the star embroidered into her shirt collar, moving toward them.

Once safely bound with the rope cuffs, a search of the man revealed two small daggers and a sharpened, likely poisoned, brooch.

"You'd better return my things just so when we sort this out," Knucklebones hissed at them as the two officers pulled him toward the cart.

"You two think you could get him back to Division for us?" Par asked the sergeant. She nodded. Zhivana recognized the woman but couldn't recall her name.

"Sure, Cordonate, we'll have them stick him in a room for you."

"Thanks," Par said.

"Where are we going?" Zhivana asked him. There didn't seem to be any reason not to take the bastard back themselves. What plan was her partner cooking up and how much trouble would it get them in?

"I'm starving and it's past midday." Par gave the snarling crime boss a nasty smile. "Let him cool his heels."

"You'll have to stop making sense," Zhivana warned him. "Or I'm going to start liking you."

His expression flicked from pained to flat. "Don't," he said.

Zhivana clenched her fists and snorted. Well, if that's how he wanted it. She glared at his retreating back and then stalked off down the alley to find her crossbow.

Zhivana licked the remaining grease from her quick lunch of lamb skewers and eyed Par. He sat on a bench in the little square near the High Courts, watching the people come and go from the various Justice buildings around them. The food from the carts set up to serve the hungry workforce was good, she had to admit that. He'd steered them to the sizzling meat and recommended the lamb. She itched to get in and talk to Knucklebones, however, and couldn't understand Par's shift from "I want to punch someone" to "let's wait and have a nice meal."

"I'm ready." She slipped off her own bench and tossed her gnawed skewers into a trash bin.

"Good," Par said. His eyes refocused and he gave himself a little shake, as though waking up from a nap. "Let's go close our case."

"Should we notify a Justicar?" Her experience was catching thieves and dealers, which they usually just hauled into the courts. The only times she'd brought on a Justicar before formal charges were for search dispatches, and they usually saw the crime in commission, or had witnesses present, and didn't have to bother with those.

"Not until we're sure. No witness, remember? We'll have to get him to confess. That's less complicated if we leave the official guys out of it." Par glanced at her and his gaze shifted to her arm. "You sure you didn't get hurt?"

Zhivana followed his eyes and realized her shirtsleeve had unrolled, the bloodstained tear clearly showing. "You see a wound?" she said casually.

His eyes narrowed but she didn't give him a chance to respond. Turning away, she started walking back to Division, rolling the sleeve back up as she went.

Knucklebones didn't smile when they entered. He'd been put in an interview room and tied to a table. At some point he'd managed to knock the stool out from underneath himself, though Zhivana suspected that he'd pissed off one of the Watch and they'd given him some help there. His perfume was cloying and tickled her nose. Underneath it she smelled sex and sweat and guessed that bathing wasn't something he'd indulged in recently.

"You crows best let me sit," Knucklebones growled.

Par shrugged when she motioned to the hunched-over man. Zhivana helped the fat man back onto the stool as Par slapped down the sketch of the broken-nosed man who had attacked them earlier.

"Don't know him," Knucklebones said with barely a glance. "I want Counsel here."

"Did you hear us charge you with anything? Why would you need Counsel?" Par said.

Zhivana leaned back against the wall and watched. Knucklebones looked upset, angry even. She couldn't detect guilt though. Then again, a man like this probably could eat a baby for breakfast and show no remorse.

"Does Nansilla Gerges owe you money?" she asked, watching his face carefully.

His muddy brown, deep-set eyes flicked to her. "Never heard of her."

"See, now we know you're lying." Par straightened up and crumpled the drawing in his fist. "Where were you last night?"

"Whoring?" Knucklebones drew out the word into a question, as though he couldn't quite recall.

"Maybe a few bruises will jog that memory," Par said, moving around the table.

"You gonna let him bleed me?" Knucklebones licked his lips nervously and craned his head to look at Zhivana.

"Not if you start remembering things," she said with an exaggerated shrug. "Help us, help yourself."

Par pulled on his leather gloves slowly, standing very close to the now-sweating man. A beaten confession wasn't unusual, but they did tend to cause future issues. Hit a man too hard and he'd tell you anything you want to hear just to make it stop. Zhivana figured she'd let Par get a few hits in before she put a stop to it. If she could.

"Heyla, no need for busting heads." Knucklebones leaned away from Par. "I ain't done nothing you crows would want, I swear. Maybe I loaned zi Gerges a few bits now and again, but she's a flower-eater. Whatever she accused me of—"

"You didn't do nothing, we get it," Par cut him off. "Tell us about her son. You loan him money?"

"Akil?" Knucklebones's confusion looked real. His face quickly smoothed and he pursed his thick lips as he realized what he'd just given away. "He budge someone over, mayhaps? Somebody important? There a stroke prize?" The idea of a reward seemed to calm the ugly bastard down.

Par glanced at Zhivana, his green eyes annoyed. She shook her head. Knucklebones seemed to genuinely have no idea that Akil was dead. Par grimaced, looking like he still wanted to punch the crime boss, or maybe just Zhivana. For a moment she wondered why he didn't anyway, but quickly realized that it wasn't restraint but mistrust. Par probably believed she'd complain if he did anything rough without cause.

She sighed, pushing away from the wall. She hadn't survived half her life policing the Levi and the

Docks because of her light touch or soft heart. If he didn't trust her to have his back, then how could she trust him? They had to start giving each other a chance at some point.

"Mayhaps," she said, echoing the street cadence. "You tell us what you know, we maybe cut you free."

"I ain't spilling 'cept there's coin."

Zhivana spread her arms out and grinned. "Pity. I'm thirsty. I think I'll go get a cup of tea or five. Of course, I might get distracted by paperwork; you know how it is with this job. I'm sure my partner will take good care of you."

The man might be terrifying when surrounded by his thugs and in his own domain, but here, tied to a table, he just looked old and sweaty and greedy as a beggar. Even the blood-red velvet of his coat had dimmed and wilted in the stuffy room.

"Enjoy that tea," Par said. He almost had an approving look on his face, but it disappeared before Zhivana could be sure.

She threw the door open but didn't set a boot outside the room.

"Bitch," Knucklebones yelled. He glared at her as she turned back around, then flicked his eyes to Par's gloved fists and swallowed audibly. "I'll tell you about Akil. I ain't talking in court but I'll give a 'davy if I has to."

"Talk," Par said as Zhivana closed the door again. "Or she goes and takes a nice, long break."

"Why do you think Akil killed someone?" Zhivana added.

"Everyone knows his mother drowns herself in smoke, most days." Knucklebones shrugged, wincing as the motion tugged on his bound wrists. He leaned slightly forward over the table and licked his lips again. Zhivana could have lived without hearing that wet smack a second time. "She used to flip her skirts, to pay. But no one will buy anymore, so she borrowed from me."

"You loaned to an addict with no prospects?" Par raised his eyebrows and folded his arms across his chest.

"Because Akil paid her debts?" Zhivana asked, though it was more to confirm. Pieces were sliding into place in her mind.

"Not to me direct," Knucklebones said, tilting his head. "But she'd show up with coin regularly enough. I figure her son took care of her. But not in the last few months. She kept borrowing and then begging off."

"So she owes you a lot of money? How much?" Zhivana asked.

"Owed. Seven suns, six seeds, rough count." He closed his eyes, speaking as if reading the figures off a page.

Par whistled and Zhivana agreed. Seven suns were about two month's salary. Little less with her promotion to Cordonate, but still, she'd always taken her wages in seeds and bits. She did the maths in her head. Fifty-six seeds to a sun meant that Nansilla had owed almost four hundred seeds.

For some people, that was easily an amount worth killing over. But the sun inside Akil's throat didn't make sense. Why waste such a coin?

"How were you expecting to collect?" Par asked. His face was troubled as well, jaw tight, and eyes worried. Zhivana guessed he had the same thoughts. She wanted the bastard to be guilty, wanted to tie a nice knot on this case, but too many things weren't making sense yet.

"Don't need to," Knucklebones said. He grinned, his teeth yellow and shining with spit. He almost looked as though he were enjoying this and drawing it out on purpose. "Boy showed up at the *Roost* a week gone now. Evened up with two suns extry to keep mama smoked."

Zhivana sucked in a surprised breath and heard Par doing the same.

"He gave you nine suns?"

"Ten, to cover the juice on the rest." Knucklebones rolled his shoulders.

"Apprentice in the treasury must pay better than our jobs," Par muttered as he turned to Zhivana.

"Not with where he was living," she said. "Even so, ten suns? I'd expect a rich merchanter to come up with that, perhaps, but an apprentice? Even if that's a month's wage, having it all at once and using it to pay Knucklehead here? With no pressure on him?"

"So you threatened him, right? Send someone around to collect?" Par leaned back down over the table, getting right in Knucklebones' face.

"Asking a man for money owed is no crime," the fat man said, leaning away as far as his bonds would let him. "But it didn't take busting nothing, I swear. My guy said Akil was calm as clams and told him he'd pay up in full within a fortnight. And he did. If he says we busted him over the money, he's lying. And it was fair debt. No law against loaning coin." His eyes darted between Par and Zhivana and she could see the gears shifting in his mind as he tried to figure out why they'd hauled him in.

"Know what I think?" Par started punching one fist into his hand, punctuating each sentence as he started talking faster and faster, leaning low over the sweating crime boss. "I think you are weaving lies out of truth. I think his mother owed and you knew an addict like that wouldn't ever pay, so you put the squeeze on her son, the man with the job. I think he refused and your guys got too rough, stabbed him over and over. I think you robbed his corpse and then left it as a message, maybe hoping to squeeze more from the widow later, eh? Is that why she was packed to leave? You have your men rough up a pregnant woman, send her running scared?"

"Widow? Who's widow? Stabbed?" Knucklebones wasn't faking that confusion, not in Zhivana's opinion. The fat man's eyes were wide and his jaw worked as he tried to follow the thread of Par's accusations.

"He didn't do it, Par," she said softly. Her partner looked two seconds away from starting to hit more than his own hand.

"You suddenly a mind reader?" Par's expression just about peeled the fur off her face. "Or maybe it's because he's such an upstanding, honest fellow. That what you're saying?"

"Akil got the money from somewhere. Maybe where he got it from is what killed him." She shrugged.

"Killed him?" Knucklebones repeated. He shifted on his stool as he tried to put distance between himself and Par's seething form. "That's what this is about? I didn't kill him. Listen to your bitch, crow. I didn't even know he was dead."

"He pulled a knife on you," Par said to Zhivana. He still looked like he wanted to hurt somebody, make it someone's fault for his case getting more complicated by the minute.

"So we book him for menacing an official?" Zhivana sighed. "More paperwork. You going to walk him over to the Courts?"

"You book me and I won't give a 'davy. If'n that money paid becomes a piece of your case; don't come to me for testimony."

"That another threat, Knucklehead?" Par looked back down at the sweating, anxious man.

"A promise. No law against not talking, either." He puffed out his cheeks and tucked his chin stubbornly into his thick neck.

"You should be Counsel, seeing as you know all the laws so damn well," Par said.

Zhivana held her breath as he paced away from the table. It was Par's call. She could see the appeal in hauling Knucklebones's annoying ass over to the Courts. Especially if they did the paperwork slowly, since he'd miss the third session and be held overnight with whatever drunks and addicts and other scum the Watch dragged in.

But if this information helped their case in the end, losing his testimony about the money paid could be very bad. Cases were made and lost in the Courts on such things, and without a witness to the murder, their chance of a solve was very low anyway. Whoever killed Akil Gerges had cared more about sending a message than the value of a sun. That many stab wounds and the coin in the throat meant this was personal, somehow. Maybe Akil had stolen money from someone close to him. If he had, they'd want Knucklebones to show where that money had gone and possibly provide motive.

"Fine," Par said through gritted teeth. "We'll send a clerk in. You tell that clerk everything you just told us about the debt and how Akil paid, and we'll see about cutting you loose for good behavior."

"These suns that Akil paid you," Zhivana said. Something was tickling in her head again, something important, an idea that refused to form fully in her conscious mind. "Were they new-minted? Unusally shiny, like my badge here?" She held it up and it glinted gold, then red, then gold again as it twisted in the light.

"No, they were just suns. Looked typical to me." Knucklebones shook his head.

Par raised his eyebrows at her but she jerked her head toward the door. She didn't want to say anything more about what she was thinking in front of the crime boss.

"Behave or you'll have a very long night," Par said over his shoulder as he followed her out.

"What was that about?" he asked as the door closed.

Zhivana walked down the hall, away from the interview rooms, and didn't stop until she reached the stairs. "Akil worked in the treasury office."

"Sure, but they don't make the coins down in Alchemy. Those guys just oversee the formulas for part of it. It's set up so no one person has access to the finished coins except the high officials."

"But he's already in the treasury building. That sun in his throat looked new. Maybe someone with access had something to do with this. Or maybe they pay the Treasury people with new-minted coins. We need more information."

"All right." Par took a deep breath. She almost admired the speed at which he could go from rage to reason. "Provided Knucklebrains is telling the truth, Akil did come up with a goodly amount of funds quickly. And we both saw no evidence he had that kind of money laying around at either his place or his widow's."

"Widow first? Or the Treasury?" Zhivana asked.

"Let's see if Jala Kawthar showed up to identify the body, then track down Akil's boss." Par started down the stairs. "After we find a clerk."

The widow was a no-show, so Par and Zhivana went back out into the lengthening shadows of the afternoon and headed to the Treasury for the second time. Clouds were beginning to roll in from over the ocean and a chill wind blew, making debris dance in the street. People went about their business hunched in jackets and cloaks with their collars and hoods pulled up.

Par jumped down from the hack and hurried up the steps, glad he'd grabbed his jacket before leaving Division.

"Smells like rain," Zhivana said behind him.

He stepped into the building, out of the insidious wind and took a deep breath. The Lieutenant was keeping his case load light on purpose, Par knew, but he still felt pressure to get this murder bagged and handed off to the Justicars. Cases without witnesses were tough. They had a couple of days, maybe, before any evidence and possibly the killer slipped away from them. It was more than likely the broken dagger they were looking for had already been thrown into the bay or the river or even sold and melted down for the metal.

Not that solving a murder would ease his heart any. No hope at all for that.

"Come on," he said when he noticed Zhivana staring at him. Par had to admit that so far she'd been pretty smart, though not having her cinch cuffs on her just made him shake his head. When she'd offered to leave the room, leave Knucklebones at his mercy, she'd made it clear she was willing to let him run this investigation his way. He supposed that was worth cutting her a little slack. A very little.

A clerk looked up as they entered the Alchemy office, raising her eyebrows. She was about twenty and wore an austere dress in the typical apprentice grey. Par flashed his badge at her.

"We want to see," Zhivana checked her notes. "Ze Batros."

"Yes, of course, please." The clerk nodded and got shakily to her feet. She looked confused and her eyes were puffy, as though she'd been crying.

"What is it, Rahli?" Fawzi Batros didn't even glance up from the book he was making notes in as the apprentice tapped lightly on the half-open door before stepping inside.

The office was long and narrow, featuring a scarred, copper-topped table running the length. It looked more like a library than a laboratory, at least to Par. He'd expected more strange equipment, maybe beakers bubbling with unknown substances and colorful smoke tainting the air. Instead the place smelled almost sterile with a hint of ink and something sweet, like apples, underneath.

"Cordonates to see you, zir," the clerk said, already backing out of the room.

Batros was a big man in his fifties with thinning salt-and-pepper hair and sleeves rolled back over muscled arms. His eyes narrowed beneath heavy brows and he wiped his hands on his leather apron before coming around the long table toward them.

"We'd like to ask you about Akil Gerges," Par said.

"I heard he was murdered?" Batros said.

"Last night or early this morning," Zhivana confirmed. "You know anything about it?"

Right. Like he was just going to fall to his knees and confess if he did. Par shook his head slightly. Zhivana seemed, if anything, a little too forthright. But he let her roll with it.

"You talk to his mother? She has some problems." Batros shrugged. "But Akil kept to himself. He was a good kid."

Everyone seemed quick to point to the mother, Par noted. First the pregnant lover, now the boss. "Akil borrow any money recently?" he asked.

"Recently?" Batros ran a hand over his scalp. "No. Took an advance on his pay a couple times last fall, but it's frowned upon. So I told him to stop asking, and he stopped." His dark eyes flicked between them. "Today was supposed to be his last day. It's a damn shame, it is."

"His last day?" This was news. Par caught Zhivana's eye and raised a brow. "He get a new job?"

Batros rubbed his hand over his scalp a second time and took a deep breath. "I'll be honest with you and I hope to the gods it helps you catch whoever did this. Akil had problems, money problems, I think stemming from his mother's habit. That sort of thing, well, technically we don't fire people over it, but this is the treasury office. We can't have people who could be easily bought or compromised working here."

Par nodded, trying to smile encouragingly though it felt flat to him. "I understand. So Akil was encouraged to quit?"

"I raised him to journeyman status so he could get another position. He turned in notice and I just assumed he had. His girlfriend, Jala? She'd know more about this."

"What was his wage?" Zhivana had her notebook out again.

Batros hesitated and then sighed again. Par had the vague feeling the man was playing up his emotions for their sake and wondered at the act. "Four suns a month, plus a stipend for continued training through the University of Science and Alchemy."

"Would he have had access to anything sensitive? Anything he could sell off? Was that a big concern?" Par tried to imagine how their victim had come up with that money and the book of alchemical formulas he'd found in Akil's aparment came to mind. He wished suddenly that they'd brought it with them so Batros could tell them what it was.

"No, not likely. This office is locked when I'm not here, and only I and the night guard carry a key." Batros looked contemplative, but again Par got the impression it was faked somehow.

"Did he bank anywhere?" Zhivana made a note.

"I wouldn't know," Batros said. "Rahli?"

"Zir?" The clerk poked her head back in far too quickly. She flushed as Par turned and looked at her.

"Did Akil bank anywhere that you know of?"

"No." She shook her head. "He drew his wage in coin each month."

"Thank you, Rahli. You can close the door." Batros gave her a look that said he was aware she'd been eavesdropping.

"He's got space down in the vault though," Rahli added. "We all do. Anyone who works here I mean."

"Did he use it?" Par asked.

"I don't know. You could go check. I mean, there're guards there with the keys at all times."

"Thank you, Rahli," Batros said again, more forcefully dismissing her. He looked suddenly agitated. "It's been a long day here, are we done?"

"Almost," Par said. "Where were you last night?"

"I was, I'm… ," Batros began, and then got even more agitated, his hands darting around like angry birds. "I was home. In bed. My wife will confirm that. How dare you even imply—"

"Save the bluster, zir." Par nodded to Zhivana. "Give her your address and we'll just check that alibi. I'm sure everything is fine if you've got nothing to hide."

He grudgingly gave his address and added, "I have nothing more to say to you. Get out."

"Well," Zhivana murmured as they walked down the hallway, following Rahli's directions to find the vault. "That was interesting."

"Maybe. People do tend to get mad when you accuse them of murder." Par shrugged.

The vault was a bust. The guards politely but firmly denied them access. Par considered threatening to go get a dispatch, but he wouldn't be able to secure one before the next morning anyway. Third session in the courts would be well underway and all the Justicars looking toward dinner, not more work.

The wind had definitely picked up and a light drizzle started as they left the Public Works building. Even Zhivana shivered, mist beading on her fur.

"No jacket?" Par asked as he yanked up his collar. "I guess this is summer weather compared to the Kurzan Steppes, eh?"

Zhivana glared at him and her ears flattened. "Wouldn't know. I'm city born." She strode off ahead of him.

Just a normal day on the job. Making friends and solving murder. Shame pricked his heart and he hurried after Zhivana with a rueful shake of his damp head.

"Parshan? Zhivana? Where are you at on this?" Hajjar leaned in the doorway to his office, a mug in one hand.

Par shoved wet hair out of his face and shook his head. "Not much so far. We know the victim came up with ten suns to pay off his mother's poppy dealer. We got stonewalled by the guards at the Treasury. Widow wasn't home, so we wasted that drive for nothing."

"Basically nothing adds up," Zhivana added. "The widow is hiding something, the boss was agitated by the idea that Akil might have had something in the Treasury vault, and we have no idea how an apprentice with his means came up with almost three months wages to pay a debt that wasn't even his, or why someone would set up a meeting, stab him a bunch of times, and then shove a coin down his throat."

"No witnesses?" The lieutenant motioned at their case board with his mug. The office was empty and it looked as though everyone else had already gone home for the night.

"Only that thug that attacked us, and we don't know how that's related."

"I wish we could find him," Zhivana added. "I have a feeling he'd have a hell of a story to tell us."

"Maybe there's some kind of inheritance, though no one mentioned any other family. We need to find Jala and talk to her again. Maybe talk to Batros more, shake him up a little," Par said. "He seemed fake to me."

"I agree," Zhivana said, flipping through her notes. Par resisted rolling his eyes at her enthusiasm. He needed to play nice in front of Hajjar, who was watching him like a concerned parent.

"Good. See what comes up with the boss and go re-interview the mother tomorrow. What about this new place the widow said they were moving to?" Hajjar asked.

"I'll check records on that. If they bought a new place, the city would have the information somewhere." Zhivana shrugged.

"If it isn't lost in paper-shuffle hell," Par muttered.

"Go home," Hajjar said. "You two can hit records tomorrow and do more digging on Gerges and his widow."

"I'll drop by Records on my way home; see if I can't get a request in early. We'll need a dispatch for the Treasury vault, but that'll wait until courts open tomorrow." Par shrugged his damp jacket back on.

"I've got to write up that report on the guy who went out the window," Zhivana said. "Night, Par."

"Night." He nodded to Hajjar, feeling the Lieutenant's gaze on his back all the way out of the building. There was more he wanted from Records. Though the fight that day in the apartment had happened fast, Par could have sworn the first arrow had hit the kirgani. The bloody tear in her sleeve backed him up on that. He clenched his hands as he crossed the square and ducked into the Records hall.

He didn't know how she'd healed, if she had. Magic, other than that given by the gods to the priests, was forbidden. If she was a bloodmage, legally he'd have to kill her. But a false accusation was also punishable by death, if proven it was made with knowledge to the contrary. He didn't want to accuse her of magic use without real proof.

He wasn't sure he'd accuse her even if he had it. He just wanted to know for sure.

If she were a bloodmage, he thought grimly, *I'd know, wouldn't I? Could I kill her? Have I fallen so far in my hypocrisy, Kalja?* Her ghost, if she had one, didn't answer.

CHAPTER SEVEN

Par finally had some luck. Numa Cham, who'd been a friend to him going back to his days in the Watch, was working the records desk. It was late in the work day, and the long, standing-height desk dividing the request room was mostly empty of people. There was a large stack of pre-printed forms at one end. He filled out the formal requests for Akil Gerges, Jala Kawthar, Nansil Gerges, and Fawzi Batros. He shook the sand into the little tray and stared down at his handwriting for a moment as though he could see right through the names to the motives and actions beneath.

But the squiggles of ink stayed silent and still on the paper. Par took the forms and waited until the last person left the desk before approaching, smiling brightly at Numa.

Her brown eyes crinkled in suspicion and she touched one hand absently to her grey bun as he approached.

"Parshan," she said. "With a smile that big, you must want something equally large."

"You know me too well, Numa," he said, taking her hand across the desk and bending down as though to kiss it.

"What do you need?" She yanked her hand back and shook her head at him. "You haven't been this friendly since before..." she trailed off as he felt the smile slide off his mouth like a rope going taut.

Par took a deep breath. The anger simmered there, but he knew Numa had meant nothing mean, hadn't meant to hurt him with reminders. But the hurt was there, always there, a wound that would never heal, bleeding him out on the inside, forever.

"I just need a favor," he said softly. "I need to know about any records for these people, the case number is on there." He pushed the forms across to her. "And, well, I'd like to see the record on a Zhivana Nedragovna."

"No form?" Numa raised an eyebrow. "Why does that name sound familiar?"

"Probably because you would have filed her transfer paperwork recently for CCD?" Par shrugged.

"Oh no," she said, nervously shuffling the forms. "You know I can't just pull files on a fellow Cordonate. Not without authorization way over your pay grade."

"Please, Numa, she's my partner. I just want to know a little more about her." He paused for a moment, almost ashamed of the card he was about to play. *Almost.* "I just want to know her record, know I can trust her, that… ," and again the pause. He bit his lip, willing his eyes to tear up a little, which was easier than it should have been. "That I can keep her safe. I can't lose another partner, Numa." Par twisted his hands together where they rested on the desk.

She sighed heavily and he knew it had worked. "I can't just give you her file." A brief pause, then she continued with a little nod. "It's late, we're almost closed. I'll put these requests on top for tomorrow and get you Nedragovna's file. But you'll have to wait until everyone has gone, and you'll have to stand here to read it ."

"Thank you, Numa."

"You're welcome, more or less. I'll be here though. Not that I don't trust you not to muck with it, but I can't in good conscience let it out of my sight."

"I understand, I won't take long." Par smiled at her, keeping it subdued this time. She harrumphed and walked off to put in his requests.

He didn't intend to mess with Zhivana's file. There were just a few things he wanted to check. Like how often she'd been in fights. How often she'd called in sick or been out injured. His suspicions said that she wouldn't have often been ill. But if she were a mage of some sort, what other markers would there be? Though he didn't want to, Par thought about his own file, his own career.

He didn't get sick much, though he'd realized after getting a few comments from buddies in the Watch that this was strange and started taking sick days, faking a minor illness at least once a year. He could control how badly he was injured or how quickly it healed, so that hadn't ever been a problem. If he'd been hit with an arrow today he'd have just left the wound there, let the medics stitch him up.

So why hadn't Zhivana? Par picked at a spot of mud on his pant leg, flicking it off the soft leather. His new partner didn't seem stupid. But if she was what he suspected, why not leave the shallow wound there instead of trying to explain it away? Do a lame job of covering it up, even.

She'd seen him looking at her torn sleeve, seen the questions in his eyes. Par had no doubt that their exchanged glance carried some meaning as she'd rolled her sleeve back up again. But had she just been telling him there was nothing to see, move along? Or was it a warning? If she knew what he was, would she reveal him to save herself? Could he kill her to protect himself? Trust her, or kill her. If she knew.

But that wasn't the real question beneath it all. *Do I care? Does it matter if she kills me?*

Don't I deserve to die?

Numa jingled keys at him as she came around the desk, waking him from his brooding stupor. "Let me lock up the office, then I'll assist you."

He just nodded. Outside the window, it had started to rain again and night was falling quickly. Par stood and stretched, watching the beads of water run down the thick glass. Then Numa returned, turning down the lamps until just a couple remained lit. The records request room took on a cavernous, ominous feel as the shadows advanced.

"I'll be right up with that file," she said.

Par leaned on the desk and watched the small, older woman descend the back stairs and disappear into the glow of light below. She came back fairly quickly.

"It was still on the filing cart, from adding her CCD paperwork," Numa said, setting the heavy file on the desk. Every incident report, every promotion, every evaluation, everything. All of Zhivana's life relating to the Watch, and now the CCD, would be in this file.

"Don't take your time," Numa muttered. She retreated, however, and started sorting a stack of papers, glancing at Par out of the corner of her eye every now and again.

He couldn't imagine this would take long. He started in; skimming for the information he wanted.

Zhivana Nedgragovna. Born in Pyrrh to an immigrant kirgani family. Parents were both dead. Joined the Watch at fourteen. Broke her left arm as a recruit in training. Assigned to the Docks and then the Levi district following the Sea Gates incident. Exemplary career from then on.

Par snorted as he read. Zhivana was a poster child for the Watch. No rumors of bribe-taking, perfect reports and response to command. Her captains reported unanimously that she was smart, tenacious, and a born leader. Their only complaints were always that she was occasionally reckless with her own life, but she'd never been injured after the arm as a recruit. Never sick either.

Married. *What?* Her file listed her married to a kirgani, Kamen Pachkovich. *Famous sculptor Kamen? No wonder she doesn't take bribes. No need for money if she's married to* that *Kamen.*

And she had a lot of official kills. Par's heart beat quickly as he got to the incident reports. A pattern started to form, a strange and very scary pattern. She'd go in with a small team to back up a Cordonate or, twice, an Inquisitor, against a necromancer or blood mage or a suspected demon. Her team would die and she'd be sole survivor. Par found the incident where she'd helped Kamilah. Some idiot had tried to perform a summoning ritual and it backfired, killing the Watch who intervened as well as the summoner himself. Zhivana was the only one who survived. Unscathed. Kamilah and her partner hadn't arrived until the aftermath.

Par unclenched his fist and forced himself to breathe. She wasn't normal. It was all here, on the page, clear as daylight. No proof, however. Every single incident could be written off as just dumb luck. Incredible, almost god-given fortune.

Well, at least we have something in common, he thought ruefully; *those around us tend to end up dead while we survive.* It wasn't enough to accuse her of being a magic-user, not formally. But come the morning, Par intended to have a very intense conversation with his new partner. She could report him for reading her file, but he doubted she would. Not with what he suspected, what he knew.

Par closed the file, rubbing his thumb over the faded ink of Zhivana's name. Tomorrow, tomorrow he would sit her down and get answers. No more lies that would kill. Never again.

"Kisa?"

At the sound of Kamen's nickname for her, Zhivana felt the mound of tension that had built in her upper back and shoulders all through the day melt away, becoming as insubstantial and unimportant as snowflakes on fur.

"I'm here, Kamenka," she called out. Zhivana slipped into their bedroom and quickly stripped off her damaged shirt. She could hear Kamen climbing up the spiral stairs from his workshop on the second floor and didn't want to answer any awkward questions about the tear in her sleeve. She'd had enough of that for the day.

As she undid her belt, something fell to the smooth wooden floor and rolled beneath the low-framed bed, glinting gold and silver in the dim light. Zhivana hung her sword up on its hook above her clothes trunk and reached for a robe.

Kamen came in as she was bent over, feeling around beneath the bed for whatever had fallen.

"Must have been a hell of a day to put you on your knees," he said and Zhivana could feel the warmth of his smile without having to look.

"Something fell," she muttered. "Ah, here it is." Her fingers closed on a hard, round disk. She sat up and opened her palm in the lamp light. "Fifty whore-poxed curses on his black shaggy head," she growled. In her hand was a shiny, new-struck sun. She didn't have to guess where it came from.

"Definitely a good day," Kamen said, leaning over her to get a look.

Zhivana slammed the coin down on the side table so she wouldn't forget it in the morning. "No, not really. My partner has a strange sense of humor."

Kamen drew her up, pushing her robe, which she hadn't even belted yet, open and running his hands over her fur. Shivers ran through her and she leaned into his strength. He nuzzled her neck and she wrapped her arms around him, ruffling his black and silver fur with gentle strokes.

"It's good to be home," she murmured. "My partner hates me, my first case is a dud, and I killed someone by falling on him. How was your day?"

"That's my Kisa." Kamen laughed, pulling her closer. He smelled good, of sassafras wood, white plaster, and tea oil, with that faint musk that was all his own beneath. "I've got a bottle of *Hamurbi Bells* red wine and two large steaks with your name on them."

"We celebrating?"

"Almost done with that pesky griffin for Lady Samurdin. She paid the rest of the commission today after seeing it."

"Ah, your new greatest work?" Zhivana pulled back from him and flopped down on the bed to remove her boots.

"That'll be whenever you finally let me sculpt you, lovely."

"You'll go to your grave unfulfilled, how sad." Zhivana wished she hadn't said that as soon as it was out. She didn't want to think about life after Kamen. It left a shadow, a growing hollow place in her heart. He was older than she by nearly five years. How many years did they have left, fifteen if they were lucky?

Kamen didn't seem to notice her renewed tension, and chatted amiably on about his commission while poking fun at the fancy Lady Samurdin and her terrible perfume as Zhivana regained composure and stripped off the rest of her clothing. She set everything into its place, making sure she was ready for the next morning and trying to keep her mind away from work, from the case, from Parshan Kouri and his inexplicable dislike of all things her.

Attempting, poorly, to keep her mind off his setting her up with that damn coin. How could he even for a moment think she wouldn't bring it right back to Division? It was like he wanted her to be crooked. Bastard. Cock-wilting, worm-eating, hairless jerk.

"Kisa? I think I'm talking to the wall. Greetings, wall, my old friend." Kamen teased her gently as she refocused and realized she was standing in their living area, staring into nothing.

"Sorry, Kamenka. Distract me." She turned and held her arms out to him.

Kamen, with a devious little smile and a twitch of his handsome silver ears, did exactly as she asked.

"Kisa, why must you keep these hours?" Kamen rolled over and watched her dress.

"It's my job. The Grave shift starts early morning. I've had worse hours. At least I don't have to work through the night." She'd lit only one tiny lamp and her husband looked like a pool of dark fur among the pale sheets.

He reached over and picked up the sun from the nightstand. "What's this about?"

"A test, I suppose. We got it out of the victim's throat." She brought the lamp over, careful not the spill the seal oil out of it, and sat down on the edge of the bed. They could afford the more expensive alchemical lamps, but she preferred the soft light and sea smell of the cheap ones.

Kamen leaned around her, holding the coin in the light. "I wonder," he murmured, flipping it over and over in the dim yellow light. "I can't figure out who made it." He sat up and used a taper to light another lamp.

"What do you mean 'who made it'?" She sighed. If he wanted to talk all morning, she'd be late again. "One of the people in the treasury."

"But which one?" He held the coin in the pool of light, his golden-brown eyes reflecting the flames. "You remember Makrina?"

"That striped bitch who thinks you should be married to someone more of your station? Someone like her?" Zhivana remembered her perfectly. She'd attended one very tense, very short dinner with Kamen a few years before and afterward bowed out of all social functions though she knew it hurt Kamen's feelings.

Kamen refused to rise to the bait, and nodded, still staring intently at the coin. "Yes. I went to a party about a month back and there were a bunch of humans from various guilds. I ended up talking to a couple of the die-cutters for the Treasury, the ones who make the coins – all the coins. They showed me a little secret, though it's not really a secret, just their way of putting their mark on things."

Zhivana pushed away her bitter thoughts and ran what Kamen was saying through her mind. Her heart started to pound and she could see the precipice again, feel the edge of important things crumbling beneath her proverbial feet.

"What marks?" she said softly.

"Grab my purse; it's over there on the floor somewhere." Kamen waved his other hand as he kept his eye on the sun, flipping it over in his palm.

Zhivana brought his purse to the bed, the black velvet soft and heavy in her hands. Kamen dumped the contents onto the bed as she lit the third, bigger, lamp. His purse held mostly seeds and suns, but there were a few larger, thick crowns mixed in. She bit back a comment on how he was carrying around more coin than she made in a year. Likely most of this Lady Samurdin's final commission payment.

"Grab a sun," he said. He pointed to Akil's coin. "Here, see how this sun has eight rays?" He took the sun Zhivana offered him. "Now look at this one – it also has eight, but see how this one is a little shorter?" She nodded, her heart still punching its way out. "The eight rays with one shorter is Anwar's signature. He's one of the four who cuts dies for the Treasury. Get another one."

One by one she pulled suns from the pile on the bed and they compared them to the coin from her case. Kamen showed her the little signature marks, tiny deviations from the standard, for each of the cutters. Deviations her coin didn't have.

"See? It's too perfect. None of the suns are perfect like that. It's a sort of in-joke at the treasury." Kamen looked at her, his ears pricked forward and eyes glowing in the light. "I don't know how they did it, but this is a forgery. A brilliant forgery."

"You can't counterfeit Pyrrh coins. The shine, the chemicals, the materials—" Zhivana trailed off as her mind leapt right off the cliff and she felt the ground rushing for her with crushing certainty: *Even if you could make the dies the right way, get the right metal composition, have the tools, you'd still need the perfect, utterly secret alchemical mix to make the coins glimmer right.* "Alchemy. Treasury office." This case wasn't about a *debt*. Pieces swam into place, locking into place around her as she ran through the case in her mind.

"Kisa?" Kamen reached for her but she stood and plucked the coin from his hand.

"I might need to use your name to get in to see this Anwar and his people, if that's all right?" She stuffed the coin into her pouch and then lifted her sword down from its hook.

Kamen nodded. "You want some of these suns to show your coworkers what I'm talking about?"

"I love you," she said, nipping his ear as she bent over and grabbed the four examples they'd found in his pile.

"Kisa," he said, hesitating as she turned in the doorway, watching him. "Whoever made these probably killed that boy to keep the secret. Be careful."

Zhivana smiled at him, showing a lot of teeth. "When am I ever careful, Kamenka?"

He sat in the pool of money and lamp light as she disappeared out the door. "That's exactly what worries me," he whispered.

Zhivana hit the street at a run. She lived down in the lower Four Bridges, not too far to walk to the High Courts. She needed to find a runner and get a message down to the docks. She had a hunch now why Akil's widow hadn't shown up, and where they might have been moving to. A runner, a message, and then, well, then she was going to go turn Par's little test back on him by breaking their case. *Serves him right.*

CHAPTER EIGHT

For the second time in as many days, Zhivana found herself taking the stairs up to the CCD floor two at a time with her sword banging her thigh. And also for the second time in as many days, she was the topic of discussion in the Grave shift duty room as she arrived.

"Enki's sake, Zhivana, late again?" Par turned toward her from where he'd been talking to Hajjar. Par looked much like a scolding mother, hands on hips, eyebrows raised. Hajjar's expression she couldn't read.

Not that it mattered. She was about to tear the whole thing apart and make this day very, very interesting indeed.

"The sun, in Akil's throat," she gasped, catching her breath as she stopped next to her desk and waved them over.

"What about it?" Par ran a hand through his hair and glanced nervously at Hajjar.

Zhivana almost let him stew for a minute. It would serve him right to bring up exactly what he'd done to the Lieutenant. Excitement won out over spite.

"It's a forgery. A fake." She dug into her belt pouch and pulled out the suns, setting them up carefully in a row on the ink-stained, scarred wood of her desk.

"No, not possible." Par came around the desk and stared down at the coins. The one from their victim was easy to pick out since it was the newest of these and still very bright in color. "It's perfect."

"Too perfect." *Don't gloat*, she warned herself, *it's not polite*. Quickly she explained to Par and Hajjar what Kamen had told her and showed them the various tiny deviations on the suns she'd borrowed from her husband.

"Wait a moment," Par said. He went over to the case board and pulled out the little box underneath that held evidence and the victim's belongings. He grabbed the notebook he'd taken from the trunk in Akil's apartment. "This look like alchemical stuff to you?"

"Stolen formulas?" Zhivana looked down at the scrawled notes. A word stood out here or there, but mostly it looked like gibberish, meaningless symbols on a page.

"Get it vetted by someone we trust," Hajjar said. His big chest expanded and contracted like a bellows as he sighed heavily. "Nothing about this goes out anywhere until we confirm it. Get someone from the Treasury down here; wake them up if you have to. We need to make sure we're looking at what it looks like we're looking at before I go bother the Captains."

"You think dayshift will try to pull this away from us?" Par asked.

"Not if I can help it," Hajjar's lips pressed into a tight, pale line and he shook his head, braids swinging.

"Dayshift?" Zhivana asked. "Why would they?"

"They're all pulled from the Guild's Watch. Othman, their captain, likes to grab any high profile cases for himself. And he's got a lot of clout with the Lord Provost and the Security Advisory Council."

Zhivana swiveled her ears toward the door as she picked up boots on the stairs. A moment later Kamilah and Hashim stomped in, damp from the morning drizzle.

"We've got bad news," Kamilah said as she stripped off her long coat and tossed it negligently over a chair. "Our floater's your perp there." She motioned to the case board and the sketch of the broken-nosed thug.

"Your floater?" Zhivana asked.

"Unfortunately. We got called in early to check out a body found floating in one of the lower canals down near the fleet wharf. Turns out it was your guy." Kamilah bee-lined for the samovar and tea on the sideboard.

"Someone sliced him a new mouth," Hashim added, making a slashing motion across his throat.

"So much for that lead." Par looked at Zhivana and something in his moss-green eyes read like a warning. *We'll talk later*, his eyes said.

Fine. If he wanted to hash out whatever the hells his problem was in private, she'd happily oblige him. She had her own things to say, starting with the damn coin and his botched attempt to get her in trouble.

Fortunately for both her and Par, Hajjar didn't appear interested in how she'd ended up taking evidence home.

"I've put a query in down at the docks about Akil and his woman," Zhivana said. "I'm thinking maybe if he were involved in a scheme like this, he'd have looked for a way out of town. Maybe planning to run is what got him killed?"

"Until we talk to the Treasury, we don't know if maybe this is just a new coin. It's possible that someone up high decided that the little cutters' marks had to stop." Hajjar laced his fingers together over his belt and nodded to Par and Zhivana. "Let's make sure all our stones are set level before we build a case on this."

"Understood," Par said. He raised an eyebrow at Zhivana. "Shall we?"

They didn't even make it to the doorway before a thin girl wearing the bright blue-and-red checkered tabard of the Runner's Guild hurled up the steps and nearly bowled Zhivana over. The runner skidded to a halt and muttered an apology.

"I'm here for a zi Nedragovna?" the girl said, eyeing Zhivana.

"That would be me," Zhivana said. She stepped back into the room and motioned the runner to follow.

"Missive from the Master of Ships," the girl said. She pulled a scroll case out of her satchel and checked the seal before handing it over.

Zhivana cracked the seal and pulled the message out. The Master of Ships had gotten back to her more quickly then she'd expected, though she'd used her acquaintance with him to advantage when writing the note.

"Well?" Par said, not quite leaning over her shoulder.

Zhivana rolled up the note and stalled a moment, still annoyed with Par for his stunt with the coin. Only after she heard him gritting his teeth did she give in.

"He's got Jala. Well, the name of the ship and captain who list Jala Kwathar and Akil Gerges as paid passengers." It was nice to know her instincts were still working. Maybe she could do this job after all.

"Good," Par said. "She's still at the dock?"

"Ship hasn't sailed. Could be she's hiding out there." Zhivana tipped the runner a bit and dismissed her.

"Let's go ask her some questions then."

"Not yet." Hajjar's voice made Par jump, but Zhivana had been aware of him standing behind them, so only turned and cocked her head at him. "I want this nailed down before I go cause headaches upstairs. Go to the Treasury first and see if that coin is counterfeit. Then go see after this ship."

"What if they sail before we get there?" Par asked.

"They won't," Zhivana said. "The morning tide is coming in; no large ships will leave the harbor 'til the tide turns this afternoon."

"Oh? And you know this well enough you'd stake our case on it?" Par glared at her.

"Parshan," Hajjar said with a warning tone. "Go to the Treasury."

Par snorted and turned away, stomping out the door. Zhivana shrugged at Hajjar who just shook his head. She followed her partner out, catching up to him as they hit the lower landing.

"I worked the docks for years," she said as she reached him. "If they sail today they won't sail until this afternoon."

Trust me, she wanted to scream at him, *I feel the rise and fall of the tides in my blood like a thing breathing in its sleep*. But she couldn't say that, not without sounding crazy, not without explaining the reason. She wondered if he would turn her in or just kill her himself. *Not that he could kill me*. Zhivana swallowed a bitter laugh.

"Fine." Par shot a strange look at her as they paused on the stoop of the Division hall. "If that widow is hiding on the ship, she's likely afraid of someone or knows more than she let on. But we'll play it the way the Lieutenant wants. Treasury first."

Zhivana nodded. She trusted Kamen's diagnosis of the fake coin, but she could see how they would need to button this one up tight with more than a kirgani sculptor as witness if it came down to a trial.

"Let's go," she said and shoved aside the door, stepping out into the chill morning.

Ze Latif, the coin-maker who showed up for work first that morning, leaned back on his stool and slowly pushed the magnifying lens away from his face. His grim, shocked face told Par all he needed to know.

"This isn't possible," Latif said slowly. "I know what I said when you came in, but, this isn't possible."

"It's a counterfeit sun for sure?" Zhivana had her little notebook out again as though she were prepared to take an affidavit right then and there.

Par resisted asking her if she were his partner or a clerk and just gave his head a little shake as her blue eyes flicked to him. She twitched her whiskers at him and he wondered if that were the kirgani way of rolling one's eyes.

"It has none of those inconsistencies, the signatures that my partner spoke of, correct?" Par asked.

"It isn't just that. See these lines? See the depth of the strike? Our dies are cut to a certain depth. It's a miniscule difference, only an expert would see the difference. But it's clear. No one in this office struck this coin." Latif folded his arms and looked Par directly in the eye. "I'd swear it in the courts if needed."

"We'll send a clerk to take a formal statement," Par said. He reached for the coin but Latif picked it up first.

"How? It's got the right tone, the right shine." He flipped the sun back and forth between his calloused fingers. "This alchemy is…" He paused for a moment, flipping the coin around and around so that it glinted gold and then silver and then gold again in under the bright alchemical lamps overhead. "This got something to do with that Gerges fellow getting killed yesterday?"

Par snatched the coin away and tucked it into the inner pocket sewn in his coat.

"We don't know," Zhivana said. "Thank you for your time, ze Latif. We'll be in touch."

"Probably safer for you if you don't mention this sun or your speculations to anyone," Par added. When the coin maker hunched up defensively and backed a step away, Par realized he was looming and turned away, avoiding Zhivana's look.

She waited until they were outside the office and the door was firmly closed behind them before she spoke.

"Threats, I've found, don't generally do their job."

"You're in the bigger game now, *kitten*, so watch and learn," Par said, deliberately using the slur to ward off his own guilt. "And put that damn notebook away. Can't you keep things inside your head?"

"Writing it down helps me and provides a record," she said, though she tucked the notebook and the inkstone away.

"You sound just like…" *Kalja*. Par bit off the name before he said it. "Nevermind. Let's go see if the widow is on that ship."

"Wait," Zhivana called after him.

Par spun and prepared to shut down any questions concerning what he'd been about to say but she motioned toward the stairs that led down to the Alchemy office.

"You got that book on you?"

"The one from Akil's place? Yes." Par patted his coat.

"We're right here. Let's go see if it is what we think it is. Another connection closed for the Lieutenant, right?"

"Ze Batros didn't seem too happy to talk to us before."

"Ze Batros won't be in this early. But his apprentice, Rahli, said plenty yesterday."

As eager as he was to get to the ship and find someone he *could* yell at, Par knew Zhivana was right. Damned if he'd tell her that though. He grunted and started toward the stairs.

Rahli was in and looked up at them with red-rimmed eyes. She didn't appear to have slept the night before.

"Cordonates?" she said, rising from her desk and wiping ink-stained fingers on her rumpled robe.

Par pulled the notebook from his coat and shoved it across the desk at her. "Can you tell us what this is?"

"It's Akil's. One of his older notebooks, see the date on the first page? He kept school notes in it, useful formulae, that sort of thing. We all have several of these around." She started to leaf through it and then stopped, blushing and glancing up at them with a guilty look. "Sorry."

"Don't be sorry," Zhivana said. She inserted herself slightly in front of Par as though to block him from view. He wondered just what his expression looked like and took a deep breath, letting it out slowly.

"Can you tell us if there's anything in there that shouldn't be?" he asked the apprentice, keeping his tone gentle. He hadn't slept much either the night before and tried to muster some sympathy.

Everyone has their grief and their ghosts.

Rahli nodded and bit her lip as she returned to leafing through the notebook. Par looked around the office, noting the charts on the walls and the frayed carpet. The place was clean but old and carried none of the sterile laboratory feel of the inner office. A light haze of piney incense hung in the air and Par noticed a smudge on the narrow windowsill where something had burned.

Pine. The scent for the dead. He gritted his teeth and looked away.

"Oh," Rahli murmured suddenly. "This is… , I mean… , oh." She looked up at them with wide eyes. She'd reached the end of the notebook and her hands covered the final pages as though by hiding them she could undo the act of seeing.

"What is it?" Zhivana leaned forward even as Par did, both peering through the girl's fingers at the symbols on the thick paper.

"It's, I think, I mean, these are recipes. For the money. Suns and crowns. They have a different formula for each and I've never seen the whole thing – that's only for masters like ze Batros – but I've seen parts for all the coins because we're taught how to mix and handle some of the more volatile parts. It's kept locked up. Nobody uses these recipes unless they need to make some for a batch of coins and then Batros locks the office and we're not supposed to even see all the ingredients he gets, I mean, he gets them all himself, but I think this list and these symbols here… , see the v with the horns? That's hartshorn and that circle with the squiggles is verdigris and that's a scruple mark for this…" She finally stopped and sucked in a huge breath. "It's a recipe. Two recipes. I think. Ze Batros would be able to tell you for sure. Why, why did Akil have this?" Her brown eyes were huge in her wan face.

"That's what we're trying to figure out, Rahli," Zhivana said. "You've been a good help."

Par thought of Batros's unpleasant, dismissive manner with them the day before and added, "We'll talk to Batros though, all right? Don't mention our visit to him until we can."

"All right," she said, ducking her head in a slow nod. "But, it doesn't make sense." She handed Zhivana the book, letting go reluctantly.

"What doesn't?" Par asked.

"Akil. He wouldn't have access to those formulae. I don't even know how he'd get into the vault to get them. Only a master can, and then only with a signed writ from Master Nibala. She's the head of the Treasury and gets authorization from the High Lord himself and the Council to make new coins. Without that, no one gets into the inner vault where the formulae are kept."

Par and Zhivana exchanged a look. It was a hole in their growing theory that Akil had stolen the recipes, but not too big of one. There was always someone careless or greedy somewhere in the chain.

They left Rahli sitting at her desk, her arms wrapped around herself, still shaking her head as though she could deny all of the events of the last couple days and right her world back to stable.

That lost look on the apprentice's face disturbed Par, threatened his safe blanket of anger and hollow apathy. He didn't want to feel, and especially not to relate. Her grief and fear gave the shadows in his heart substance, and he didn't like the form they took.

"Now can we go to the stupid ship?" Par said. He'd meant it as a joke, but it came out sounding more petulant than joking.

"Yes," Zhivana said softly. "I'm curious what sort of coins were used to pay this Captain Mahbod Soroush."

CHAPTER NINE

The *Dreams of Nin*, Captain Soroush's triple-masted, caravel-class trading vessel, was docked at the end of Pier Five. The gentle sounds of water shifting beneath her feet and the pull and creak of ropes and aged wood calmed Zhivana as she and Par made their way down the long docks. She'd trod these boards for years, checking ships, bantering with captains and crew alike, the sea wind ruffling her fur, the smell of fish, salt, and seaweed clinging to her clothing.

Sounds of shouting carried down the ramp as they neared the ship, and she exchanged a look with Par, both of them loosening their swords as they moved up the swaying ramp toward the unseen commotion on deck. Sailors were gathered around a bearded man wearing a captain's red sash and a younger man whose clothing was richly embroidered and well-tailored. The younger man's face was unveiled, which was a good sign. At least they weren't dealing with a lordling. Likely he was a merchanter, since he wore no guild patch or medallion.

"Heyla!" Par called out as they stepped off the ramp. "CCD! What's going on?"

Zhivana kept an eye on the sailors. They looked more amused than riled, but were still tense and wary, ready to draw blade for their captain if the mood turned. They shifted to the sides, leaving space for her and her partner.

"This boy is disrupting my ship," the captain said, waving a hand at the young man.

The man in question turned and seemed about to yell at them, but stopped as he saw their medallions and their hands on swords. His eyes widened almost comically and his hand went to the velvet purse tucked in his belt.

That's interesting, Zhivana thought.

"Name?" Par asked.

"Danu Almasir. There's no trouble here that needs a crow." His voice shook, belying the strong words.

"He's trying to take back money fairly paid," Captain Soroush added. "And bother a passenger besides."

Following her instincts, Zhivana asked, "Would that passenger be one Jala Kawthar?"

Danu shifted his stance, looking like he was thinking about running, but there was nowhere to go except over the side of the ship, as she and Par were between him and the ramp.

"Aye," said the captain. "There trouble here?"

"Do you have the coins ze Almasir paid you with?" Par asked.

The captain nodded, his eyebrows knitting together. He asked two of his men to go fetch both their passenger, Jala, and the black velvet purse in his strong box.

Danu threw up his hands in an exaggerated gesture and tried to walk past Zhivana. She put her hand on his arm, gripping hard enough to make him wince. "Stay put," she said through her teeth. "We might have questions for you."

She supposed it could be complete coincidence that this young man was looking for their widow and acting this nervous besides, but years in the Watch had taught her that coincidence was a pretty poor assumption when it came to crime. Danu backed off, yanking his arm out of her grip. He reached for his belt again, this time for something that wasn't there. A crease in the soft leather belt told Zhivana that a knife sheath of some sort used to rest there. This situation grew more interesting by the moment, and she smiled, letting her teeth show.

Jala, looking scared and exhausted, appeared, helped up the stairs from below decks by one of the sailors. She saw the young man and real terror seized her face. She stepped behind the sailor, as though ready to use his body as a shield.

"Zi Kawthar," Zhivana called out, drawing the young woman's attention to her. Jala seemed to relax a little when she saw the two of them, but she moved slowly, her arms wrapped around her belly and her eyes darting from Zhivana to Par to Danu Almasir.

"Captain," murmured another sailor as he handed over a velvet purse.

The captain tossed the purse to Par. At the same moment, Danu kicked out at Zhivana, forcing her to jump back a pace as he lunged forward, ripping the purse from Par's hands even as her partner caught it. With a yell, Danu ran for the seaward side of the ship, ripping his own purse from his belt as he went.

Zhivana and Par both ran for him, sailors shouting and trying grab the young man as well and all of them getting in each other's way.

Danu threw the purses over the side, the red and black velvet bags landing in the green water with a double splash. He turned toward them, grinning with his hands in the air.

Zhivana didn't stop to consider anything. Her belt came off, her weapons thunking onto the smooth planks as she dove past the smiling Danu and over the side of the ship.

The chill of the water hit her with a thousand icy needles through her cloths and fur but the sea song woke in her blood, its singing welcoming and warm. Ears flat, nostrils pinched shut against the salty water, Zhivana kept her eyes open as she kicked her way deeper with her powerful legs. She let her normal senses go, concentrating on what the sea was telling her, on the feel of the currents which were sluggish here in the harbor. The purses would have gone almost straight down, so straight down she swam, arms out, seeking.

"Bloody hells," Par muttered.

"If she drowns, that's none of my problem," Danu said. The smug smile was gone from his face, wiped clean by Zhivana's insane dive off the ship and by Par's bruising grip on his arm. "You have no call to keep me here."

"If she drowns," Par said, "you're next."

"That was a threat!" Danu squawked, looking at the captain and sailors all leaning over the side of the ship, staring at where the kirgani had gone into the water. "You all heard him threaten my life."

"I heard nothing more than the water against the side of the ship," Captain Soroush said. The dozen or so sailors gathered at the side all shrugged or nodded, following their captain's word.

"There!" One sailor pointed and Par turned. Zhivana's head broke the surface of the water and then her fist followed, gripping both purses as she treaded water. The men scrambled for a rope ladder to get her back onto the ship as she paddled toward them.

The relief Par felt burned in his throat, warring with his anger at her for going over in the first place. He added it to the list of things he wanted to talk to her about. Later. They had far more interesting problems at the moment.

"You," he said to Danu, "are coming with us. And so is the widow. I have a feeling you all will have interesting stories to share about what we're going to find in those purses."

Captain Soroush had refused to hold off on sailing that afternoon, though he'd offered his men for the unloading of zi Kawthar's things from the ship. A clerk had been sent to take his statement for the record about the purse and how it had come to him. It was better than nothing.

Which was what both Jala and Danu were saying, each stashed away in an interrogation room below.

Ze Latif had been brought in from the Treasury, since he already knew about the counterfeit coins. Par paced around the duty room while the coin maker examined each of the suns found in the two purses and slowly divided them into two piles. Tension sat on Par's shoulders like angry monkeys and anticipation made his head hurt. They were so near to closing this case. He wasn't sure when he had transitioned from wanting to have a closed case on his record to help show he was back and doing fine to wanting to close *this* case in particular. Maybe it was Akil's mother's grief resonating with his own hollow pain;, maybe it was the terrified, unhappy look of the suddenly silent widow.

That the little bastard sitting in an interrogation room being babysat by his partner while awaiting counsel seemed so sure he would escape justice for his multiple crimes probably didn't hurt, either. Hajjar hadn't been entirely happy that Par and Zhivana had hauled in the second son of one of the most wealthy merchant families in Pyrrh without a writ or even notifying him or a Justicar.

"Ten counterfeit suns in the black purse, eight in the red. The other coins are genuine." Latif stood up and tucked away his magnifying lenses. "Same die as the one that cut the coin you showed me earlier. I can tell from the depth of the indents."

"Good. Thank you," Par added, remembering civility. They would need this man to testify.

"What disaster of a case are you all foisting on me now?" a deep voice cut in.

Par turned and smiled wanly at Justicar Majid. He was a middle-aged man with a big voice, big chest, and a shrewd, narrow gaze. Par had never seen him dressed in color, the Justicar choosing to wear tailored suits of black, white, and grey exclusively. His curly hair was cut unfashionably close to his big head and he wore silver rings in the tips of his ears, his only jewelry besides the chain that held his badge.

"Majid," Par said.

"Parshan," he replied, smiling faintly. "You have a suspect I should see?"

"Aye," Par said. "We should go see the Lieutenant first. I'll give you the short version on the way."

"I'll go find a clerk to take my statement?" Latif asked, brushing off his vest.

"Ah, yes. Thank you," Par said. He'd almost forgotten the Treasury official was still there as his mind had shifted to how to best tell the story of the case to the Justicar.

Hajjar still looked annoyed when they found him outside the room where the widow, Jala, was being held.

"Justicar," he said, nodding in greeting to Majid. "Par fill you in?"

"Aye. Thin case without a witness. We might be able to get the boy on having and using counterfeit money, but without witnesses or a confession, I don't see murder sticking."

"I spoke with ze Deeb, the High Officer of the Treasury. They want to keep this as quiet as possible."

Par raised an eyebrow at that but knew he shouldn't be surprised that Hajjar had been dealing with things behind his and Zhivana's backs. Something as big as counterfeiting Pyrrh coins would of course trump the murder of an apprentice. He shoved down his annoyance, telling himself that this case was just a case. If it got solved, it got solved. If not, well, solving or not wouldn't bring back Akil and nothing short of that would help the widow or zi Gerges with their grief.

Par knew that all too well. He'd personally killed the man who murdered Kalja, and it hadn't done a damn thing to help. So much for justice or closure.

"That seems smart," Majid said. "The widow talking?"

"No, she insists she knew only that Akil was getting money from somewhere and that he wanted to leave town and move on. She claims she had no knowledge of Danu Almasir's involvement with her man, didn't know that he'd paid for her passage, and that she'd never seen him before today."

"Which is wormshit," Par added to Hajjar's statement. "I saw her face when she came onto the deck. She was terrified. She knew him."

The lieutenant gave him a warning look. "If she won't speak up, we can't do anything about it. She's not a suspect in the murder and the ship captain's statement confirm that the coins paid for her passage were from Danu Almasir, so we can't hold her for the counterfeiting either."

"So we're down to the kid. I want to talk to him." Justicar Majid shrugged his wide shoulders.

"Counsel is with him," Hajjar said. "But I've got a Cordonate sitting in as well."

Par didn't miss the look that passed between Hajjar and Majid that clearly asked why Par wasn't the one sitting in and was answered with a look that said "you know why." He followed the two men down the hall to where they were holding Danu Almasir, trying not to feel like a spurned pup scampering behind his masters.

Between his status as a merchanter's son and having Counsel present, they couldn't afford to have him go rough on Danu Almasir, even if Hajjar or the Justicar would have allowed it. Knowing Hajjar almost like a father, and Majid nearly as well, Par thought they might have let him get away with a little punchy intimidation, but it was far too late for that now.

Even Zhivana looked like she wanted to scrape the smug half-smile off the young man's face with her claws. Her shirt and trousers were still damp from her swim in the harbor and her calico fur stuck out from her head and neck at scruffy angles. She watched Majid's pointless questioning with flattened ears and a tight jaw.

"I don't know where those coins came from." All Danu's answers were the same, full of "I don't remember, I don't know." He claimed he threw the purses overboard because he didn't like the looks on the Cordonates' faces, claimed they had threatened him and he was worried they would try to plant something on him.

"That's enough," said Counsel Goli, a trim, elderly woman with a tidy grey bun and a flat expression that said she had heard and seen it all. "I told his family we would be down at the courts for second session. Justicar Majid and I can work out the charges on the walk, yes?" Her tone was as bland and bored as her face.

"Yes. I'll meet you and ze Almasir out front." Majid waited until the Counsel and Danu had left before spreading his hands in apology at Par and Zhivana. "We've got him for dealing in counterfeit coin, which could mean time in the mines and a huge fine. There's no evidence for murder here, or for actually making the coins."

"What will the treasury do about that?" Zhivana asked.

"Cordonate?" Majid paused, having not been introduced to Zhivana.

"Zhivana Nedrogovna," Par supplied. "My new partner."

Majid raised his eyebrows and gave her a quick once-over, taking in her scruffy appearance and probably a lot more, but his expression quickly smoothed and Par couldn't guess what his thoughts were. "They will tighten security, do an internal audit, and change their formulas. We can all hope that the counterfeiting began and ended with Akil Gerges."

"You believe that, I've got a canal to sell," Par muttered.

"Enough." Hajjar glared at Par. "Hands are tied. This case is out of our purview."

"Fine. I'm coming along to the court though." Par looked at Majid and relaxed a bit when he nodded.

"Me, too," Zhivana added. No one argued with that either. For maybe the first time since he met her, Par didn't even feel like trying to push her away. She'd put up with him for two days now, jumped off a ship to try and make their case. He didn't see the point in fighting with her anymore. He was too damned tired.

Even the momentary satisfaction was all-too-brief when Danu saw them walk out with the Justicar and that smug smile slipped right off his idiot face.

It seemed the whole Almasir family turned out for the court appearance. The father, Zhivana assumed, looked like an older, heavier version of his son. Like the rest of the small crowd of dark-haired, richly dressed men and women, he wore his wealth on his person in jewels and embroidery, reminding her of the sunbirds perched on the outer pylons in the docks, spreading their golden feathers to attract mates.

The father seemed to be spreading his feathers to gain favor for his son. He spoke to the judge passionately about his son's character and how there was no way he could have known the difference between the real coins and the fake ones.

"We're not here to argue the case, ze Almasir," the judge said with a pained look. "Just to decide on the date for the trial and if," he glanced down at his notes, "Danu Almasir should be held in custody or released."

"The crime is non-violent, your honorable zir," Counsel Goli said. "His family is willing to make assurances with collateral that Danu will appear."

"There might have been a murder involved in this case," Justicar Majid pointed out. His voice was deep for a human's and pleasant to Zhivana's ears. He and Par seemed friendly and their body language spoke to a personal relationship. Another piece of subtext she would just have to wait to find out the meaning of, Zhivana supposed.

"There's no evidence or witnesses that connect Danu to the murder," Counsel Goli said, pushing down on Danu's shoulder as he tried to rise and speak.

"Is that true?" The judge asked, looking at Majid.

Majid sighed. "Yes, honorable zir." He looked no happier than Zhivana felt, which was cold comfort now.

"Very well," the judge looked over at the clerk. "Put them in the schedule for next week. We'll have appropriate copies sent to the Justicar and Counsel. Danu Almasir is given over to familiar custody, pending a collateral of fifty suns held by the court."

It seemed a steep amount to Zhivana, but ze Almasir didn't argue. She guessed, for their family, it was nothing. Compared to the lives damaged by their son, maybe it *was* nothing. He certainly seemed to be getting no more than a finger shaken at him. Spending of counterfeit money? What was the penalty for that? A fine? She glanced at Par and saw her own frustration mirrored in his tight jaw and unhappy eyes.

Danu Almasir looked over at them, his smug smile back in place. Par casually drew his hand over his throat, as though to scratch at the two days' of dark stubble growing there, but his cold green eyes made the gesture clear enough. Danu's smile slipped a little and he jerked back around.

"That the end of it?" Zhivana asked Par softly as they slipped from the courthouse and headed back across the square toward headquarters.

"That's the end of our part of it. No evidence or witness for our murder, nothing more to do. Now we write up our report and file the case away." Par's words were clipped and his fists were clenched so that his normally brown knuckles now looked white and bloodless.

"No chance of getting a writ to search Danu's home, eh?" Zhivana said it more for herself than to him.

"Not bloody likely. If he were lower class, we could just do it and take the slap on the wrist." It was clear from Par's words he'd been thinking the same thing. "But as it stands, it would cost us our jobs at best. It's clear we're being told to back off."

"Is it?" Zhivana asked as they approached headquarters. She raised her hand to wave in response to Lieutenant Hajjar's own curt wave. The tall lieutenant had obviously been waiting for their return.

Par's head snapped up. "Zir?" he said, his surprise making him sound almost polite.

"Walk with me," Hajjar said.

Though the sky threatened rain, the air was almost still. Delicious smells from the food carts almost drowned out the normal city smells and Zhivana's belly remembered that she hadn't eaten in many hours. Hajjar didn't seem to have lunch on his mind, however.

"It's obvious you two don't want to let this go and let the Treasury handle it," he began in a low voice as they walked on either side of him around the edge of the square. "I don't blame you. It's clear to me that boy is either our killer, or covering for our killer."

"His belt had a mark on it, like mine gets when I take my sword sheath off," Zhivana said. Par nodded, adding that he'd noticed this as well.

"Your murder weapon is likely long gone," Hajjar said. "But a counterfeiting operation would take tools and chemicals. It has to be somewhere. I'm going to give you both the rest of the day to yourselves." He waved off their protests. "Let me finish. I wouldn't be unhappy if you both spent that time in the Hall of Records, looking into the history and holdings of the Almasir family. I'll write you a note to clear your access without formal requests."

"And if we find something interesting?" Par asked.

"In that case," Hajjar said with a bright grin, "Majid is going to have a few more headaches."

Zhivana and Par spent the rest of the morning and afternoon pouring over records. It amounted to little, only adding to their frustration. There was maybe enough, and a slim chance of a maybe at that, that they could convince Hajjar and Majid that the Almasir family was worth prodding.

Zhivana stretched and looked back at the inky scrawl of her notes. The family had first risen to status through spice trading up the coast, but had accrued an unhealthy amount of creditor debt filings after two of their ships were lost in the last Great Storm a couple years back. The debts had all been paid, not so quickly as to raise suspicions, but quickly enough to raise Par's eyebrows and have him point it out. Since then, they'd expanded their shipping into more areas of trade and built three more ships.

"It's a lot suspicious coincidence with no proof of anything," she muttered.

"Numa's giving us the 'I want to go home' eye," Par said, replacing another stack of folders on the cart next to him.

Zhivana craned her head around to look at the friendly, elderly human clerk. She was, indeed, giving them the eye, and her smile at Zhivana had an edge of tried patience in it with more teeth than a kirgani would have shown a friend.

"We can bother Hajjar with what we found tomorrow and maybe the Justicar can get us a sympathetic judge." Par stood and shoved his hair out of his eyes.

They walked out together into the evening drizzle. The food carts were shut down and huddled forms ducked in vain from eave to eave as people left the High Courts, heading home or toward the eateries, tea houses, and taverns.

"Which way are you headed?" Par asked her. "We could share a hack; escape a walk home in the wet."

The offer surprised her, but Zhivana tried to keep it hidden. She wasn't sure how to take this new, calmer Parshan, a man extending the ring of peace and maybe even friendship. She also realized she had no idea about his personal life. Where he lived, who he might live with, if he had family or anything.

"I live down to the west, off Blue Square," she said. "It's not a long walk. You?"

"Ah, I live east, practically over the canal just on the other side of Stonebridge."

"See you tomorrow then," Zhivana said, unsure if she should offer her hand.

"Tomorrow." Par turned up his collar and walked away without saying more.

She hadn't realized how tired she was until she started home through the misty streets, dodging carts and other pedestrians. It was more than just her frantic morning or the long swim down to retrieve the purses in the harbor. It was more than exhaustion weighing her bones.

It was disappointment. Which made Zhivana feel silly and naïve. She knew that a lot of investigative work was running around, looking at records, talking to people, and not all sword fights and dangerous hunts for demons, bloodmages, and child rapist villains from the half-bit papers the street hawkers loved to sell for evening reading.

But she'd solved her case, more or less. And the killer was going to walk away after paying a fine. It wasn't... fair. Or just. It was frustrating and tiring. She had struggled to fit in with an angry new partner who didn't want her, navigated her way through her first days on this job, found the man who killed the victim, and it all amounted to a lot of not very much.

When the next body came in, she'd do it all again. The idea the same result could happen stung. It was reality, she knew that in her head, but as Kamen would gently tell her if she managed to put any of these thoughts into words for him, what she knew in her head didn't matter two bits to her heart.

Zhivana told herself they would catch the next killer. Which might be true. Maybe it was true just enough to keep Kamilah and Keen and even Par doing their jobs, day in and out. Maybe in the end it would all be enough for her, as well. Today, however, it wasn't enough.

She could see the steps to her door now. No lights were on, which meant Kamen wasn't home quite yet. All she wanted was a hot bath and then maybe she'd convince him to take her out to her favorite eatery. A huge tagine of stewed fig, apple, and rabbit or flat eel and a steaming mug of spice wine to drown herself in before she went to bed and drowned her frustrations in her Kamenka's gentle arms. That's what she wanted.

The crossbow bolt took her in the chest, slamming her backward onto the cobblestones and stopping her heart. It didn't even hurt.

CHAPTER TEN

Dying was like blinking, only when her eyes snapped open again, Zhivana felt the pain she'd missed out on. Her heart was trying to beat, the muscle clenching and rejecting the thick quarrel lodged in it. Her whole chest felt as though it were on fire. She reached up and gripped the bolt, her only thought to yank it free.

"Enlil's arse!" Boots approached and a dark shape, a human man's voice, the scent of garlic, assailed her senses. Passerby? Or assassin?

Assassin. He drew a curved knife even as she twisted the bolt free from her chest, her vision blurring with tears and her throat raw as she tried not to scream. The man leapt at her. He was either shaken by her coming back to life or not very good with a blade.

Maybe both. Didn't matter. Zhivana threw the bloody quarrel at him and rolled sideways, getting her powerful legs beneath her. He slashed again and she sprang into him, knocking them both to the ground, her claws unsheathed and slicing deep into his knife arm. They rolled and she snapped at his neck with her teeth. He jerked back, trying to disengage and his arm went lax. She yanked on it, hoping he would drop the knife. He didn't, trying instead to turn it in, toward her body.

For a moment, each half on top of the other, they played a close-quarters tug of war. Then he screamed, twitched and went still, his own knife sticking from his sternum.

Her vision slowly cleared as she lay in the street, half tangled with the dead man. Her heart wasn't just beating again; it was trying to stage an escape from her chest. The alley was quiet. The drizzle cooled her face, tickled the fine hairs inside her ears. Only then did she notice that the alchemical street light that should have lit her door and the approach to it was dark. He'd been lying in wait.

She struggled to make her mind start working again. Someone had just tried to kill her. Usually there was a reason for that.

Zhivana shoved the man's body off her own, spitting out a mouthful of blood. She went through his clothing quickly. He was dressed like a tavern tough – dark shirt, filthy leather pants, simple vest, worker's boots that had seen much better days – and stank of garlic and cheap rice wine. Tucked into a thieves' pocket in his left sleeve was a scrap of paper with her house number on it and a single coin.

A new-minted sun.

Par. The odds weren't ones she'd wager on that the Almasirs, or whoever hired this killer, hadn't hired another for her partner. Men desperate enough to kill anyone for the shine of gold were easy enough to come by.

Ripping her shirt so that the hole didn't look quit as conspicuous, she ran for the nearest Watch station. They'd have a horse standing by and be able to send someone over to secure her home and the body. It was best he'd died in the fight; she couldn't have let him live even though now they'd never know from his own lips who hired him. Hopefully the coin would be testimony enough.

She knew both the Watchmen on duty and though they looked at her blood-smeared body with wide eyes, they snapped into action as she breathlessly laid out the bones of what was happening. Even on good days, Zhivana didn't like horses and they felt about the same for her, but the stocky bay only snorted as she leapt onto its back, kicking it toward Bridgeway, toward where Par had said he lived.

As she rode, visions of her surly partner danced in her brain. Par laying on a wet street, the rain running off his brown skin and into staring, vacant green eyes as blood seeped out around a crossbow quarrel like the one she'd taken in the chest.

Instead she flew across Stonebridge, the horse's roughened shoes slipping on the wet surface as she yanked him to a stop near a gaggle of Watch in russet and green milling around beneath alchemical lamps.

Par was there, in the middle, talking to a Watch sergeant. Zhivana felt like whooping in relief, but slid silently off the horse instead and shoved her way toward Par.

"Bloody hells," Par was saying, running a hand through his soaking wet hair. He looked undamaged. Beyond him, two Watch officers were standing over a cuffed human male who was dressed much like Zhivana's assailant had been, though this one was a good head taller and far larger in girth. The man was kneeling and blood trickled from his left temple.

"You all right?" Zhivana asked.

"Am I? Gods yes. What happened to you?"

Zhivana looked down at her ripped shirt and the pinkish stains. One of her breasts was almost completely uncovered. She dragged the ripped material up toward her neck and met Par's eye.

"Man tried to kill me. We fought over his knife. He lost. You got yours alive?" She motioned at the cuffed man.

"Yeah. It was amateur hour, fortunately for me. Guy figured he was so big, he could just jump me." Par gave her a wan smile. "This is going to be a lot of paperwork."

"Least you got to punch somebody first." Zhivana returned his smile, a sudden, deep tired setting into her bones.

"Maybe later, too. You should clean up. This guy will stew down at headquarters for a while," Par said. "I've got runners out to get the lieutenant."

She thought about bristling over him telling her what to do, but decided she didn't care. "Here," she said, handing him the sun and the note she'd taken from the assassin. "My guy had this on him. Get it into evidence for me?"

"See you in an hour?" Par said, though he shifted it to a question at the last moment.

An hour. So much for her bath, her tagine, or a night curled up with Kamenka.

"Sure," she said.

Zhivana had returned the horse to the Watch, scrawled a note for Kamen, pulled on a clean shirt, grabbed a rain-proof cloak, and jogged her tired way back to headquarters well before the hour was up. The drizzle had taken care of most of the rain and the ME cart was in the process of rounding up her victim's body. Hopefully they'd be long gone before her mate got home. It was one thing to know your wife put herself in harm's way every day, it was another to come face to face with a man she'd killed on your own doorstep. Par had waited for her and now they faced the man who'd tried to kill him.

The would-be assassin licked his fat lip and tugged at his cuffed hands, rattling the chain that held his hands fixed to the interrogation room table. Blood and sweat trickled down his bruised face and his fear was tangible enough Zhivana could taste it in the stuffy air inside the small interrogation room.

"I need a healer, me head's about bled out," he whined. His manner had been surly ever since he'd arrived, only his darting, terrified eyes giving away his awareness that he faced the noose for his actions.

"You'll get a healer, maybe. But first you talk about who hired you to kill me." Par leaned over the table, snarling in the man's face.

"Nobody. I was jus' trying to roll you. For coins. I swear't." It figured he was taking this line. Robbery of a public servant would mean some time in the mines. Attempted murder meant death. A big, strong man like this would see a few years hard labor as a small price for his life.

"Trying to rob me? When you had more coin on you than I'm carrying?" Par slammed one of the shiny, new suns down. It glittered between them.

"I'm greedy," the killer said, his voice back to surly now.

Zhivana glanced at Hajjar. The lieutenant leaned again the wall, watching without a word. He looked annoyed.

She knew the feeling. She stepped up to the table, gently resting a hand on Par's shoulder and pushing him back so she faced the killer now, looming over him as best she was able.

"Way I see it," she said, "there are two stories we can play here. One, you didn't know you were being hired to kill a Cordonate and you give up who hired you, cooperating with us. That might be mitigating enough for the Justicar to recommend life in the mines instead of the long drop."

He licked his sore lip again and blinked blood and sweat out of his eyes. "Or?"

"Or I guess you got hurt a lot worse in that struggle than we thought." She didn't dare break her gaze to look at the lieutenant for approval. He'd stop her if he needed to, if she was crossing a line. "I'll give you to the count of twelve to think this over."

She unsheathed her claws in silent count, one by one by one. His eyes darted between her claws and Hajjar. No one said anything.

Until she got to nine. "Life? In the mines?" The whiny voice was back.

"Ten, eleven," Zhivana said.

"Heyla! I'll spill."

"Give us a name." Hajjar spoke, his voice soft and deep and deceptively calm to Zhivana's ears.

"I don't got a name. But," the man added hastily, "I can describe him, even pick him out. Young, good looking fellow, nice teeth, rich clothes. Found me an' me friend down at the *Dusky Wave*. Said there'd be another fifty suns like the one he gave us if me and my friend took care of a couple problems. We was supposed to wait with crossbows, but I forgot mine. Figured I could take a single crow with me knife." He looked at Par. His mouth turned down and a crease formed between his bushy eyebrows as though he still couldn't quite believe that the smaller, far more slender man had bested him and knocked him cold.

"We'll get a sketch artist in to take the description," Par said, giving the man a tight, mean smile.

"Give over a nub and scrap and I can do better'n that," he said. "He came in one of those fancy carts, with curtains and a symbol on the side. Me mum always said I could've got to University with my art if I'd focused. I can draw it good for you."

Turned out, he was right about that. The emblem took rough shape beneath his scarred, bruised fingers.

"I'll be damned," Par muttered. "We have them."

"Get a clerk here and a sketch artist. No one comes into this room before he gives his statement officially." Hajjar clapped Par and on the shoulder and nodded at Zhivana. "I have to go give Majid that headache now."

"What about me deal? A healer?" The man called out.

"They're coming, depending on you staying helpful." Par sat down on a stool, staring at the emblem.

"I'll fetch runners for the clerks," Zhivana said, anxious to be out of the cramped room now. She wanted to run straight over to wherever the Almasir family lived and rub this in their smug human faces. But there were rules they had to play by. At least those rules were now working to their favor.

"Wait," the man said as she stepped out the door. "You're the one Colle was sent to kill, yeah? Funnyfurred was how the man described you. You the one? Where's Colle?"

"He have a garlic chewing habit and a big nose?" Zhivana said, looking over her shoulder.

"Aye?"

"I killed him." She closed the door behind her and took a deep breath of the somewhat fresher hallway air.

Only fair, she added silently, *he did kill me first.*

CHAPTER ELEVEN

"He's locked himself in his room." Ze Almasir glared at Hajjar, his hands tucked into the sleeves of his black brocade evening jacket.

"If you don't have a key, we have to break his door." The lieutenant's voice was calm, far calmer than Zhivana felt. Next to her in the opulent vestibule, Par was almost vibrating with tension.

It had taken until well past the dinner hours to get a Judge in to approve a search writ for the Almasir estate. Justicar Majid, looking like he had the headache the lieutenant had said he would, had managed to use the testimony of their would-be assassin and the wealth status of Danu Almasir and his family to press for immediate action. Now they were barely inside the door of the large house in Lake Market, being stalled by the indignant father.

"Is he even here?" Par asked. "He left this house at least once today already without supervision, against the advice of the court. Or maybe he wasn't unattended?"

"What are you implying? He snuck out which is not our fault. My son is of age. He has been confined to his rooms since, and now refuses to open the door, even for his poor mother."

"He'll open the door for us," Hajjar said. "Show us to his room. Now." The lieutenant's face was as hard and unreadable as one of Kamen's onyx carvings and ze Almasir's blustering tide broke against it.

Danu did not open the door for them. And when Ze Almasir used a key from a fob inside his robe, they discovered that Danu wouldn't open a door ever again.

He lay on his bed, a huge, carved four-poster with thick, blue silk-velvet curtains that matched the comforter beneath his lifeless body. His face was peaceful, only a thin skim of pink froth on his lips disturbing the appearance of slumber. Zhivana knew he was dead from across the lushly carpeted, well-lit room, his body holding that certain stillness.

He'd written a confession, neatly, as though it would be assessed by a tutor later. After ze Almasir dragged his shrieking wife from the room, Hajjar read the two tidy pages aloud.

Apparently he had devised the plan along with his friend Akil Gerges to sell the formula for Pyrrh suns and crowns to various criminal elements that Akil knew through his mother.

"As though he would run in the same circle as Akil," Par said with a snort.

They had made a few suns as testers and spent them around to see if anyone would know the difference. Then, according to Danu's confession, Akil got cold feet and wanted to leave the city. He demanded money up front so he could leave, which Danu gave, but then Danu had second thoughts, worrying his accomplice would reveal him. He stabbed him at their final meeting. He apologized as well for the hiring of the killers to take out the Cordonates, saying he was desperate because they wouldn't let it go and terrified his deceptions would bring disgrace on his family.

"I am not able to live with myself upon reflection of my actions. All the blame is mine. I am so sorry." Hajjar stopped reading and shook his head.

"You believe this?" Zhivana nudged the heavy crystal glass that had apparently contained the poison their suicide victim used to take his life. A small wax paper packet with a trace of acrid-smelling orange powder rested next to the glass.

"Where are their materials?" Par asked.

"I don't know." Hajjar rubbed the bridge of his nose. "Fetch the ME. We'll sort this out down at headquarters." He waved both of them out of the room.

"I don't like this," Par muttered.

"Did you see zi Almasir's reaction to her son's body? It was like the dramatic scene from a street play." Zhivana looked down the dark paneled hallway, but the Almasir's and all their staff had vanished.

"We'll see," Par said. He shook his head and led the way out of the house.

The grave-shift duty room at CCD headquarters felt dim and empty this late at night. Par and Zhivana waited alone, sitting at their desks without speaking, while Captain Inaya, two older humans in well-tailored jackets from the Treasury Office, and Lieutenant Hajjar talked in his office. Zhivana slumped her head on her arms, her mind spinning with the new pieces of the case, pieces that likely wouldn't matter if they couldn't get the higher-ups to listen. Her ears twitched as she tried to pick up on the voices inside the other room, but they were speaking far too low and she wasn't ready to sink to overt eavesdropping by standing in front of the door.

Finally they emerged and Hajjar looked like someone had stepped on his foot and refused to apologize. He shook his head as Par and Zhivana rose, warning them not to stop the men and woman leaving. The captain, a small, compact human woman of about fifty, with iron grey hair and iron hard eyes, paused as she walked by them.

"Good job, both of you, on closing this case," she said without a smile. "You can go home."

Closing the case?

"But," Zhivana started to say. The captain gave a tiny shake of her head, looked back at the lieutenant with a raised grey eyebrow and strode from the room.

"It's done." Hajjar said.

"What about the information we found in records? What about the mysterious wealth that the Almasir family came into?" Par folded his arms, his face an unhappy mirror of Zhivana's thoughts.

"I said it is done. The Captain and the Treasury are satisfied with the confession. This case has racked up enough bodies." That last was said with an intense look at Zhivana.

She flattened her ears and dropped her gaze to her boots. She'd killed two men in about as many days. Lovely first week on the job, for sure.

"I know it is difficult to accept this outcome, but a confession is more than we had this morning. Go home," Hajjar said with a soft sigh. "I want you both in early. There are a lot of reports that need to be written."

"That his way of saying we're benched?" Zhivana asked Par softly as they walked down the dark stairs side by side.

"Pretty much."

"You don't like this outcome any more than I do," she pointed out.

"It's the job, Zhivana. It's more than asking questions and beating up bad guys. There are politics and decisions far over our heads. You'll get used to it."

They slipped out the doors and she rattled the handle, making sure it had locked behind them. The rain had stopped and the cobbles of the square sparkled in the glow from the streetlamps.

"Are you? Used to it, I mean."

Par popped his collar and ran a hand through his hair in a gesture that was becoming familiar to her. "Not yet." He walked away without looking up, his shoulders hunched. She watched until he became just another shadow before turning and walking with heavy steps toward home.

CHAPTER TWELVE

Par sprinkled sand over his signature and sat back in his chair. It was well into the afternoon and he and Zhivana had the duty room to themselves for the moment. The rain clouds were gone and sunlight filtered into the room, highlighting the dusty windows and warming nothing.

He looked over at his partner. It was still odd to see her at Kalja's desk, but today the pain of it was less than before somehow. Maybe because he'd been staring at the empty chair for so long now that seeing it filled was something of a relief. He had to admit, if only to himself, Zhivana had held her own these last few days. She'd fought off multiple attackers, been with him question for question and thought for thought through the whole investigation. He had grudging respect for her for not wanting to let it go, either.

While they'd filled out their reports in near silence, asking each other minimal questions and making almost no small talk, Par read the unhappiness in her strange blue eyes every time they looked up at each other. This was, as Hajjar had pointed out, a slightly better outcome than that Danu boy getting a fine and walking away, but it wasn't justice or closure.

Not that closure was real. Par wasn't sure he believed in the concept. He'd killed the man who had taken Kalja's life and felt no better for it. It hadn't brought her back. It hadn't turned back time and let him make new decisions, let him throw his life in front of hers and use the power that would condemn him. Let him decide to trust instead of hesitate and watch her die.

"Who is going to notify Akil's family of the outcome?" Zhivana asked, pulling him away from his angry reverie.

"What? Oh. The courts, I suppose." He met her gaze and raised an eyebrow, seeing the thought that might have been forming behind her question. "Or, I suppose, we could. We know where the mother and widow live, after all."

"And if the widow feels like talking now that ze Almasir is dead... , well, I believe someone told me the other day that there is no law against talking." Zhivana smiled with only a hint of teeth.

"No law against listening, either," Par said, returning her smile. He looked over his shoulder at the lieutenant's half open door. "We should probably not disturb him with something so trivial."

"Get your coat; I'll meet you down after I hand this stuff to the clerk for copying." Zhivana rose, lifting her sword belt from the back of her chair. Par noticed she didn't have her hand crossbow today, remembered her asking about requisition forms for new equipment. At least she had her cuffs.

"Mother or widow first?"

"Mother," Zhivana said as they slipped out of the duty room. "It'll give us plenty of time with zi Kawthar. For listening, I mean."

They were definitely thinking the same thing. It had been clear the widow was holding back. She'd tried to leave the city and recognized Danu Almasir on the boat. It might not be something they could re-open the case with, but Par knew the whole story hadn't been told. If someone else was getting away with murder or treason, he wanted to know about it.

Well, damn me to Annunaki, he thought, *I actually care about this case.* He might be broken, but maybe he could mend.

Nansilla Gerges had been dead for at least a day from the look of her bloated, sallow corpse. Insects buzzed in the sickly, sweet-smelling vomit that had dried in the bedding around her mouth.

"Overdose?" Zhivana asked, trying not to breath at all. Decay, feces, and vomit had not improved the miasma of filth in Nansilla's run-down room.

"Kido will have to tell us for sure, but it looks that way." Par spoke through his sleeve, squinting his eyes as though that could help fend off the stench.

Zhivana squinted. It didn't help.

"Lot of lives ruined by this murder," she said. She didn't voice the thought that they might have been among the last to see this poor wreck of a woman alive.

"Death does that." Par's voice was flat and he waved her out of the room. "Not everyone can live with grief."

Zhivana almost asked him then, asked what had been between him and his old partner, but she swallowed the words along with a much needed breath of open air as they exited the repurposed inn. Par had been cordial to her all day and she had no desire to have him close off again or turn his anger back onto her.

They waited in silence for the Watch to bring the ME's cart.

"Hajjar isn't pleased you two are out here," Kido said. The anuran's scales glittered in the waning afternoon sunlight as she stood by, overseeing the removal of Nansilla's body.

"You come along to tell us what we know?" Par asked with a half smile.

"I needed some air and sunlight. Too many bodies on my table these last few days."

Zhivana turned half away, flicking her whiskers. She'd put a couple of those bodies there, and while she didn't feel much at all about the killing of those men, she regretted adding to the burden of anyone she worked with.

"Poor woman," Kido murmured. "I remember her. We had to hold her down after she made the ID on her son."

"Put me down as payer on her sheet, will you?" Par asked.

Turning back to them, Zhivana cocked her head to the side, studying her partner. He must have felt her gaze and looked over, shrugging.

"She has no one else to pay for the burning or buy her pine and prayers," he said with a too-casual tone.

"You two going with us?" Kido asked, looking between them with a speculative, but otherwise inscrutable anuran expression.

"No, we've got to tell the widow about how things came out. We'll be back soon for Hajjar to steam on in person."

"I won't bother telling you to stay out of trouble. Either of you," she added with a look at Zhivana. "But be smart."

The triangular open area in front of Jala's townhome was filled with people and carts and they had to disembark their own cart across the way. Par sent Faris and the cart back to CCD, telling him they didn't know how long this might take or if the widow was in, so they would hire a hack for their return. As they approached the heavy wooden doors, one swung open and Jala, a black velvet cloak wrapped around her body making her look a little like a licorice treat, stepped out, glancing furtively around.

Zhivana caught Par's arm and pulled him back into the shifting crowd. He started to protest but caught sight of the widow and nodded.

Jala pulled up her black hood and waved down one of the hacks that had just dropped off a neighboring woman and two young girls. She handed the driver something and they set off.

"Wait? Or follow?" Zhivana said, making it clear in her tone that she'd prefer the latter.

"Sad you even ask," Par said.

The hack went toward the wide throughway of Bay Road, heading out of the Sciences and toward the docks. The streets were crowded as some shops closed and taverns opened, more and more people spilling into the streets on their way someplace else. It slowed the hack Jala was riding in, which was a blessing to Zhivana's tired legs, but it also made it difficult to keep sight of their quarry at times.

The traffic let up as they crossed into the docks proper. Here the roads turned more to alleys between two and three story wooden warehouses that perched over the myriad canals. Zhivana moved silently beside Par and listened to the feel of the water around her, breathing in the briny air as the incoming bay water mixed with the canals.

"What in hells is she doing out this way?" Par muttered as they ducked around another building as the hack had turned left ahead of them.

"Meeting someone?" Zhivana knew it would be a lot to hope, but the widow had lied about enough things.

For all they knew, she had been in on the whole scheme. She'd had a nice townhouse, good furniture, been proud when she spoke of Akil being a journeyman. The widow wasn't someone who wanted to settle in life, not in Zhivana's opinion. She wanted the good life, wanted more than she'd had. Who knew to what lengths that kind of greed might have taken Jala.

The cart halted ahead and they hung back. The wind off the ocean kept whatever words were being exchanged between Jala and the driver from Zhivana's ears, but it was clear the man wasn't happy leaving a pregnant woman alone in this place so close to dark. Zhivana pressed her back into the rough wood of the building behind her and watched impatiently as the driver finally pulled away.

Jala waited until the man was out of sight and then moved around the side of the next building. Par and Zhivana shadowed her, keeping to the lengthening shadows. The widow tapped on the door and it opened almost instantly.

Zhivana caught only a glimpse of the man's face, but recognized him immediately. From Par's unsurprised snort beside her, she knew he had seen the man's face as well.

It was Fawzi Batros, Akil's employer, and head of Treasury Alchemy.

"Hope he isn't killing her in there," Par muttered. For having been the one to suggest they wait a few counts before going in after the widow and breaking up whatever this was, he wasn't waiting patiently. Zhivana almost wished he would go back to counting under his breath instead of rocking from foot to foot beside her.

"You want to go? Let's go," she said. She itched to draw her sword even though nothing about the situation seemed to warrant it yet. Call it instinct, she thought. Batros had been hiding things from them as well during their investigation. She'd practically forgotten about that with all the excitement.

A crash sounded from the warehouse, the pitch of it sharp, like a glass chandelier had fallen.

"All right. Let's go."

They burst through the door, Par first, both with swords drawn. The interior of the warehouse was dim, lit only by a few storm lamps and Zhivana blinked as her eyes adjusted, watering from the chemicals in the air. It tasted acidic and slightly sweet and made her nose twitch.

The room in front of them was split by a long table piled with alchemical equipment – beakers, pans, heatstones, bottles, and other things Zhivana didn't recognize. Beyond that she could make out a stairway leading up to a platform that formed the second floor of the small warehouse.

Near the table, Jala menaced Batros with a broken bottle, but both had turned when Par and she burst through the door.

"CCD. Give it up, both of you." Par called out.

"You brought the crows on me?" Batros growled at Jala.

"I didn't bring anybody," she said. "Go away. This is none of your business."

"Jala!" Zhivana cried out warning as Batros took advantage of the widow's distraction and lunged for her.

He got his arm around her, whacking away the broken bottle and brought a small but wickedly curved knife to her throat. The bluster seemed to rush out of Jala then and she went from looking angry to terrified.

"Grab the lantern, bitch," Batros growled at her. Then to the Cordonates, "Keep your distance. Me and her are leaving."

Jala took one of the lanterns off the table, the flame inside dancing as her hands shook. Zhivana and Par moved very slowly forward.

"You are making it worse," Zhivana said. "We know about the family." Which was only sort of a lie. "The Justicar will cut a deal." Probably not, alas, a lie.

"Forgery is treason. Treason means the axe. I'm not stupid, ratling." Batros dragged Jala up the first few steps.

"How's he going to get out that way?" Par asked very softly, his lips barely moving.

"Fire escape, I think," Zhivana replied, almost as softly. Most of the buildings in this area had narrow iron stairs or ladders leading down in case of fire since none of the warehouses boasted windows.

They kept moving forward, the sweet, acidic smell growing stronger as they neared the table.

"That smell," Par said. "I know it. I smelled it at Kalja's burning."

Zhivana looked down at the floor. The boards were shiny, as though they'd been mopped recently.

Igneal. An alchemical compound that burned hot and long, turning bodies, even bone, to ash, which was why the priests used it for funerals, covering the acidic smell with pine incense.

Batros had reached the middle of the stairs. Even as Zhivana and Par looked at each other, both realizing what the place was soaked in, Batros slammed the pommel of his knife into Jala's temple. Zhivana leapt forward, crossing the table in a bound. Batros yanked the lamp out of Jala's limp hand and kicked the unconscious widow down the stairs.

Then he threw the lamp into the igneal-soaked floor.

Zhivana sprang through the flames as they rose around her. Par was on her heels, cursing loudly.

"Get the widow! I'll get Batros," Zhivana yelled to him above the sudden roar and crackle of the flames. Acidic black smoke billowed around them. She couldn't hear or see if Par made a reply.

She scaled the steps in three huge leaps, sword ready. Smoke choked her lungs and obscured her vision. The second floor was dark, even her keen eyes picked up little.

Movement. She brought her sword up just in time to block Batros's swing as he came at her from the smoky darkness with a heavy board clutched in his hands. She kicked out and he stumbled back. She lunged with her sword but missed, and the swing of the blade carried her to the side as she struggled for balance on the rough, uneven floor. The noise from the growing fire ruined her hearing and Batros nearly had her again as he came out of the darkness at a new angle.

This time her sword stuck in the hard wood, locking them together. She put both hands onto the hilt, trying to force Batros back or yank the board from his grip. He was strong, far stronger than she would have assumed from his build. He outweighed her as well and slowly forced her back until she felt the railing behind her.

She tried to spit in his face, but missed. Abruptly, he released the board. The sudden lack of pressure against her threw her off balance and she stumbled to the side, clutching the thin wooden railing with one hand. It gave way with a screech and Zhivana fell back and out toward the raging fire below.

Par grabbed Jala as Zhivana leapt up the stairs. The pregnant woman had seemed slight except for her large belly, but as dead-weight, it was like carrying a pile of wet clay. The heat and smoke warred with the air he desperately sucked in as he dragged the widow up the steps. There was no way he could get her back across the room. He couldn't even see the table anymore through the smoke and flames.

Jala coughed and struggled and he tried to sooth her. She must have realized who he was, for she stopped struggling and started crawling up the steps, half-supported by his free arm.

Then Zhivana screamed. Par hauled the widow up the last few steps and she slumped over.

Batros stood on the edge of the platform where the railing had given way. Part of that railing now leaned out, suspended over the conflagration below, Zhivana hanging from it by her claws, her body outlined by the angry firelight.

"No closer!" Batros yelled. "Throw your sword into the fire."

Par pretended not to hear him and walked forward, sword out, trying to judge the distance. The floor boards were buckling from the heat, the wood sweating oil, and his boots threatened to slide out from under him.

Batros leaned over and slashed his curved knife across Zhivana's hands. Par's partner screamed again. She was struggling to get her feet up, back onto the platform, but the sweating wood was too slick and she was hanging out too far.

"Toss away the sword!" Batros yelled again. He stabbed his knife down, inches of the blade slicing into Zhivana's left hand. She let go with another angry, pained cry. "One paw left," Batros snarled, holding the knife up.

Par threw his sword off the platform.

Batros backed away, disappearing into the smoke and shadows. Par ran forward, grabbing for Zhivana's good arm. He nearly slid from the edge himself as he tried to brace and pull her back up. He knelt down, wedging the toes of his boots into cracks in the boards as best he could, spreading his legs to form a stronger base.

"I got you," he said even though he couldn't hear himself think over the crack and roar of the flames. "I got you." Her left arm was too slick with blood for him to grip and she didn't dare release her right hand from the railing. Par leaned out as much as he could, grabbing for her shirt collar. They were almost face to face as he twisted and tried to pull her in and up, back to safety.

"Par!" Her eyes widened, looking beyond his head as she cried out.

Par turned his head in time to see Batros emerging like a demon from the smoke. He swung a thick board at Par's back, ready to knock them both down into their own personal hell below.

Time slowed. Batros moved as though the air had turned to black molasses. Par saw his choices laid out before him with sun-bright clarity.

Let go of Zhivana and roll to the side, saving himself.

Letting Zhivana go meant she would fall. Die.

Or take the chance, this crazy second chance. Trust and act. Use the power even now murmuring in his blood.

Zhivana was no Kalja. But she was alive where Kalja was dead. He couldn't go back and save his love.

So he chose to go forward.

The power in his blood became a violent song in the space of a thought. Skin parted on his neck and he formed a dart of his own blood, at once flowing, then solid. Then flying straight into Batros's throat.

The alchemist stopped cold, looked surprised for a moment as blood poured from his neck, and then dropped dead with a heavy thunk that Par felt more than heard. With barely a half-thought, Par closed the wound in his own neck.

He turned his attention back to Zhivana, not meeting her eyes as they struggled together and got her back onto the platform.

"Jala?" She yelled.

The widow had fallen unconscious again, and it took both of them to get her to the hatch that led onto the narrow iron stair. The air outside wasn't yet clogged with smoke and Par had never been so happy to breath in the stale canal scent before. The three of them stumbled away, the widow awake now, coughing and spitting soot from their mouths, the smoke streaming upward behind them. The deep tones of the fire alarm bells sounded in the distance.

A safe distance away, Par collapsed against a low, stone wall. Zhivana helped Jala to sit, using both her arms as though nothing had happened. She caught Par's eye as he looked at her hands, her fur there dirty with soot and ash, but unblemished and whole.

Jala coughed again and looked at them. Tears ran down her face in grey streaks.

"I'll tell," she said and her voice was rough from the smoke and emotion. "Almasir. Batros. I have Akil's journals. I'll testify. I'll tell you everything."

"Case closed," Zhivana said softly.

Par met Zhivana's eyes, then looked away, focusing on breathing in clean, sweet air. They sat in near silence, neither quite looking at the other, and waited for the cavalry to arrive.

EPILOGUE

It was well past the midnight bell when the knock on his door, which Par had been expecting, broke the silence in his small apartment. He'd gone home after they gave statements to an annoyed lieutenant and confused Captain. He bathed and put on fresh clothes.

It wouldn't do to be arrested and executed looking like he sifted funeral ashes for a living.

If Zhivana turned him in. She hadn't said a thing about how Batros died, just that they'd fought with him and, to her knowledge, he hadn't made it out. Par went along with that story. Maybe she was waiting until he wasn't around, afraid he'd attack if confronted. Maybe she would go for the inquisitors instead of telling Hajjar.

So he waited with only a single candle lit, listening for the knock that would seal his fate.

It was Zhivana, but she was alone. In her hands were not weapons, but a dark brown bottle sealed with green wax and two pewter cups.

"Time we talked," she said.

"You're alone."

"You sound surprised. Fair, I guess." She walked past him and set the bottle down, drawing a small knife from her belt. She smelled of some kind of floral soap and her clothing was clean. It seemed like she had spent the last couple hours doing the same as him, only maybe without the 'waiting to die' parts.

"Nice place," she said with only a hint of irony as she cracked the seal on the bottle and looked around. "Apparently you hate chairs?"

He'd moved here after Kalja died and gotten rid of all their things. He wanted no reminders.

"I usually sit on the floor," he said, accepting one of the cups, which was half full of a clear liquid. "What is this?"

"Kajinori. Anuran liquor. Sipping stuff only, it's strong."

He sipped and choked. It tasted like salt water, but only at first. Then his tongue caught fire but even as the sensation hit, it faded and there was nothing left but a sweet aftertaste. Par took another sip. "Interesting."

"So," she said, sitting down cross-legged on his floor, her back against one of the undecorated walls. "First, thanks for saving my life. Second, you're a blood mage."

Par took the candle off the table and set it on the floor nearby before sitting down and leaning against the wall next to his partner.

"Aye," he said. "That going to be a problem?" He didn't look at her straight on, but watched her face from the corner of his eye.

"You going to turn into a demon?"

"Not planning on it."

"Then we don't have a problem."

He sipped the Kajinori and thought about that for a moment. The next words were hard to say, but he wanted them out. "I didn't trust her. My old partner. I could have saved her, like I saved us today. I wish…" he trailed off.

"You two were married?" Zhivana said and the understanding in her voice made his chest tighten more.

"Not officially. But she was my life. My everything."

They sat in silence after that, sipping the strange liquor. When their cups were empty, Par rose and got the bottle. He filled their cups again and then looked down at Zhivana.

"What are you?" he asked. "I know I didn't hallucinate those wounds today, but here you are, unscathed."

"I don't know," Zhivana said as he sat back down. "No really, I don't," she added as Par snorted and raised an eyebrow.

She took a deep breath, let it out slowly.

"You hear about how I was dared to scale the sea gate?"

Par nodded.

"It was stupid. I'd met Kamen already, a few months before and things were getting serious, more serious than I'd ever been. I knew I'd have to stop taking the risks I loved in my youth, so I went for one last dumb dare. And I failed."

"But you lived," Par prompted when she was silent for too many breaths.

"I don't know. That water, the current out there. It just sucked me out and down and down and I thought my chest would explode. All I could think was that I wanted to live, wanted to see Kamen's smile again, feel the softness of his fur against my face. Then there was light and warmth and I could breathe. So much light. You ever been out to the Silversmoke Isles, away from the city?"

Par nodded, thinking about the shell-gathering trips with his mother, back in better times.

"You've seen the phosphorescence then, that light that comes over the waves in the deep of night? It was like that, only magnified, like all the stars had come in close to me. And I heard this voice in my head, asking me how much I wanted to live, to go back to the surface. I begged that voice for life and it offered it to me, for a price. For a favor."

"What favor?" Par stared at her, caught up in the strangeness of her story.

"I don't know," she said with a half laugh. "That's the damnedest part. I have no idea. Some favor in the future. But ever since, I can't get hurt, not really, it just all heals right up. I don't get sick. I don't think I'm aging either, which is the worst part. And I hear the sea all the time in my mind; I can feel the tides inside me. So I don't know what I am anymore. I guess some ancient power beneath the sea has no concept of what life is to a mortal, so it just inserted its own definition."

"That's... ," Par started. Stopped. Shook his head. "So," he said finally.

"Now we know about each other, I guess," Zhivana said.

Par raised his cup and smiled, inclining his head slightly. "To secrets?"

"No," Zhivana said. "To partners and cases properly closed." She twitched her whiskers at him and smiled without teeth.

"To partners," Par repeated softly as their cups clinked.

They sat in the flickering shadows a long while and drank in silence. The candle flame guttered, found fresh wick, and burned on into the night.

* * * * *

ALSO BY ANNIE BELLET

The Gryphonpike Chronicles:
Witch Hunt
Twice Drowned Dragon
A Stone's Throw
Under Fountain
Dead of Knight
Gryphonpike Chronicles Volume One: The Barrows

The Chwedl Duology:
A Heart in Sun and Shadow
The Raven King (Coming Soon)

Short Story Collections:
Till Human Voices Wake US
The Spacer's Blade and Other Stories
Gifts in Sand and Water
River Daughter and Other Stories
Deep Black Beyond

ABOUT THE AUTHOR

Annie Bellet lives and writes in the Pacific NW. She writes the Gryphonpike Chronicles series and her short stories have appeared in magazines such as GigaNotoSaurus, Digital Science Fiction, and Daily Science Fiction as well as multiple collections and anthologies. Follow her on her blog at http://overactive.wordpress.com

21218556R00111

Made in the USA
Middletown, DE
22 June 2015